"Are you okay?"

Maggie's gaze met Jack's and she burst into laughter.

She finally managed to say, "I thought things got easier as you got older. That I'd have all the answers. Where is this wisdom, the settled lifestyle of the middle-aged woman?"

She spread her arms. "Since I turned forty, I feel like I got shot out of a cannon and I don't know where I'm going to land." She closed her fingers around the gift. "But for some reason I wouldn't have it any other way."

Jack raised the camera and snapped her picture.

"Why'd you do that?"

"Forty suits you, Maggie Moran. You've never been more beautiful, more competent, more caring, more charming. You're an incredible woman and I love you more now than ever.

"I just have no idea what the hell we're going to do about it."

Hi, Everyone!

Okay, here we go! It's time to be FORTY & FABULOUS! I'm so excited about the three books in this miniseries: *A Fabulous Wife*, *A Fabulous Husband*, *A Fabulous Wedding*.

I've always wanted to write the older hero and heroine, deal with their lives, their trials and triumphs, which are so different and much more fun, exciting and rewarding than those that come with being twentysomething.

Meet Maggie, BJ and Dixie, best friends who are all turning the big 4-0, and the terrific heroes, Jack, Flynn and Nick, who make this the time of their lives.

Visit Whistlers Bend, Montana, for fun, sass and a whole lot of romance. Life really does begin at forty. What a ride!

Yippee!

Dianne

P.S. I'd love to hear from you. Visit me at DianneCastell.com or write me at DianneCastell@hotmail.com.

— Forty & Fabulous —

A Fabulous Wife

DIANNE CASTELL

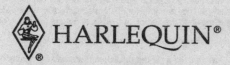

HARLEQUIN®

TORONTO • NEW YORK • LONDON
AMSTERDAM • PARIS • SYDNEY • HAMBURG
STOCKHOLM • ATHENS • TOKYO • MILAN • MADRID
PRAGUE • WARSAW • BUDAPEST • AUCKLAND

ISBN 0-373-75081-1

A FABULOUS WIFE

www.eHarlequin.com

Printed in U.S.A.

To David Anthony, the best, smartest,
most handsome son ever! I'm so proud of you!

To Beverley Sotolov,
for her help and guidance in this series. Thanks, Beverley!

Books by Dianne Castell

HARLEQUIN AMERICAN ROMANCE
 888—COURT-APPOINTED MARRIAGE
 968—HIGH-TIDE BRIDE
1007—THE WEDDING RESCUE
1047—A COWBOY AND A KISS

Prologue

Sweat beaded Jack Dawson's forehead. His stomach clenched. The red LCD numbers on the timer clicked backward. Thirty seconds to make up his mind before this sonofabitch blew sky-high, taking the First National Bank of Chicago and him along for the ride.

What the hell was he doing here? Forty-one was too old for this. He was a detective, a hostage negotiator, not a damn bomb expert...except now. How could the bomb squad be caught in gridlock on Michigan Avenue?

Dammit all! *They* should be here looking at the bomb, not him! He thought of his son, Ben, graduating—by the sheer grace of a benevolent God—next week in Whistlers Bend, Montana. He couldn't miss that. He thought of Maggie, his ex. Had it really been ten years since he'd seen her? She always hated his being a cop. *At the moment he wasn't too thrilled about it, either.*

What was that bomb-squad rule? Always cut white, the white wire? He remembered Maggie's blue eyes. Maybe it was time for a change. He held his breath, muttered a prayer, zeroed in on the blue wire...and cut.

Chapter One

Jack uncurled himself from the white minivan. Three hours ago he'd left Billings, Montana, crossed the Yellowstone River and driven to Whistlers Bend, under sunny skies and surrounded by mountains that seemed to go on forever.

That was good because the terrific weather and spectacular scenery had made the driving easy...and it was bad because his parents had insisted on stopping to photograph every mountain peak, pine tree, brook and critter along the way. He'd never dreamed that buying them a digital camera for their grandson's graduation could be so...time-consuming.

"Oh, Jack," his mother now said in a gush as she slid from the passenger side and waved at the town. "What a perfectly darling place with all the cute little shops and stores. There's a square."

She turned to her husband as he climbed from the back seat. "Don't you feel like you're in that *Horse Whisperer* movie, Edward? They even have a saloon with neon signs in the window and a diner called the

Purple Sage. We should all buy cowboy hats and get our pictures taken with a buffalo."

His dad nodded. "And put it on the Christmas cards, Gert, and enclose a family newsletter." He slapped Jack on the back. "Can't believe you haven't been here for ten years, son. This is terrific."

Jack thought of himself in a cowboy hat and shuddered. "It's not exactly my bag, Dad. Here the Cubs are bears, not a ball club, and ranch isn't something you put on salad. I don't exactly fit in."

And that was true, but the main reason he'd stayed away was *Maggie.* Immediately after their divorce he'd visited Ben every few months, but three years of also seeing Maggie had made him realize that the only way to get her out of his head and heart was to get her out of his life. That had meant flying Ben to Chicago and staying the hell away from Whistlers Bend. And it had worked until—

Oh, boy.

"Look," his mother said. "There's Maggie now, crossing the street at the next block."

Suddenly, thirteen years and all Jack Dawson's great decisions vanished like a pickpocket into a crowd. His heartbeat kicked up a notch and his chest tightened. He watched Maggie walk down the sidewalk and old feelings stirred his gut.

Maggie looked good. Better than good. Better than he imagined, though he tried not to imagine her at all.

His dad chuckled. "She still has that same fast walk. Turning forty hasn't slowed her down any. She always did things at warp speed. Sometimes made me feel like I was standing still, and I was a cop in good shape." He hitched himself up tall. "Not in too bad of shape now."

Jack raked a hand through his hair. "Yeah, same old Maggie."

"Don't know who you're watching, son, but this Maggie is not *old*."

And she wasn't. Not one bit. Nice curves. Woman curves. She walked past Pretty in Pink, Anna's Apothecary, the Purple Sage Café then into the sheriff's office.

His mother frowned. "I don't think she sees us."

Edward said, "I don't think she's even looking for us."

Jack turned to his mother. "You did phone and tell her I decided to come two days early, and you were coming with me, instead of flying in next week, because your house was getting painted?"

She tsked. "Of course I did. I had a nice conversation with Ben and he said that was *sweet,* which I assumed meant good and has nothing to do with sugar. He said he'd tell Maggie and she'd call back if there was a problem. And I said that was *sweet.*" His mother tipped her chin. "No square grandmothers here. I can do the lingo. Anyway, Maggie never called back, so everything must be…sweet."

Jack felt his eyes widen. "Ben? You told Ben? Mom, he graduates in a week. He has a girlfriend who's two years older than him and who's a high school dropout. He plays baseball instead of studying and has senioritus so bad we weren't sure there'd *be* a graduation. His brain is sawdust, the rest of him hormones. You should have talked to Maggie, or maybe her dad. Henry would have passed on the message."

His mother straightened her spine; his dad frowned. They gave Jack their best our-grandson-is-perfect look.

"All right, all right." Jack held up his hands in surrender. "I'll find out what's going on. Maybe Maggie got the message and just didn't expect us this early." Though a one-hour trip from Billings that had turned into a three-hour trip could not make them early for anything. "You two get something to eat over at the Purple Sage. It's been a long, long ride."

Edward slid the van door closed. "Good idea. You and Maggie could do with a few minutes alone after all these years. And those wide-open spaces made me feel sort of empty. I'm in the mood for pie. Henry's always bragging about that lemon meringue pie he gets at the Purple Sage."

His mother hooked her arm through her husband's and winked. "Then we'll buy cowboy hats." She pointed. "There. I see a shop called Horn to Hoof. Bet that's the place to go. This is just like a John Wayne movie."

They turned toward the café and Jack rolled his shoulders. Welcome to ten days of the Dawsons' Wild West Show. Dropping in on Maggie unexpectedly after thirteen years was not what he wanted; doing it with his parents in tow was a double whammy. What should he say after all this time? *Surprise! Guess what…I'm early.*

Oh, they talked on the phone every few weeks or so, but mostly about Ben and his performance—or nonperformance—in school. Nothing personal. Cop stories were the last thing on her mind, since being a cop is what had driven them apart. Cattle were not exactly his bag unless served up with steak sauce.

They'd led separate lives just as they'd wanted, the cop and the rancher's daughter. *Until now.*

He jaywalked without cars and buses screeching to a halt or drivers yelling colorful expletives and flipping unmistakable hand gestures—a part of Chicago he didn't miss—and entered the gray clapboard building with white shutters. Maggie was saying to the thirty-something deputy behind the desk, "Well, Roy, did you find him?"

Her thick curly auburn hair swayed across her shoulders and Jack recalled those curls sliding slowly through his fingers.

The thirty-something deputy glanced at Maggie and grumbled, "You're back *again?*" He frowned and dropped his pencil onto his desk littered with papers. "Give me a break, Maggie. I've been a one-man band around here since Cyrus's appendix exploded last week."

She leaned across the desk, her denim skirt flowing over her nicely rounded backside. Jack's mouth went dry and his hands got clammy.

"You have to find Andy!"

The deputy motioned at his desk. "This is a ton of paperwork. When Cyrus was here, he did it, but now I have to or the state gets pissy. They start calling, wanting this report and that one. Andy could have gone off someplace. He's done it before. Maybe he's not missing at all and you're going wacky over nothing."

"This is important!"

"Lots of things are important." The deputy stood and snatched a paper from his desk. "New stop signs in front of the schools." He held up another paper. "Anti-drug programs." He snagged another. "Out-of state truckers speeding on the back roads near Silver Gulch, when we don't get truck traffic in these parts."

"Ride out with me tonight. We'll look for Andy and the truckers. Do that and I'll help you with paperwork and sheriff things tomorrow, I promise."

Huh? Jack's jaw dropped. "You're helping a *sheriff.* Going out with *him* when you divorced *me* for being a cop? *Like hell!*"

Maggie spun around, her blue eyes big as a full moon over Lake Michigan. Their gazes collided, and for a moment all thoughts other than Maggie Moran—once-upon-a-time Dawson—left his brain. Fresh, honest, determined…lovely. Like the first time he'd seen her twenty years ago, a student at the Art Institute of Chicago, sketch pad in hand, hair blowing wild, eyes bright and blue and exciting and…

This was no time for a stroll down memory lane, dammit. And he should have forgotten all those things.

He thumped his chest. "You left *me* because I chase the bad guys and now you're going out with a man who does the very same thing? Thanks a lot!"

JACK? HERE? NOW?

Broad shoulders, chocolate-brown eyes, always brave, a hero and still the most drop-dead gorgeous man on earth. *But not here now!* This required a period of adjustment, like the time between now and when he was *supposed* to show up.

She remembered the last time she'd seen him, splattered with blood after a shoot-out. Something inside her snapped like a rope pulled too tight and she knew she had to leave or go crazy. "You're…early."

Oh, brilliant! How often had she thought about seeing him face-to-face again and what she'd say? Sometimes late at night, her throwing herself into his arms and telling him she was sorry she'd left seemed the way to go.

Other times, usually after she'd heard of some lifethreatening escapade in Chicago that involved Jack Dawson, she wanted to tell him he was a damn fool and she was glad she'd left.

Jack stood with his legs apart and arms folded and studied her. "You can't be serious?"

His words brought her back to the present. "I have the date circled on the calendar. The sixteenth. Two days from now is the sixteenth."

His eyebrows drew together. "Not *that*—the part about helping out a sheriff. You had a fit every time *I* went to work and now you're doing this! Call in the FBI. They're the ones responsible for missing persons and have all kinds of resources."

"Persons?" Roy laughed, bringing Maggie's attention to him. He stroked his jaw. "That's a good one," he said to Jack, and sat on the corner of his big oak desk, knocking papers onto the floor. "The missing

Andy is a bull. And not just any bull. A buffalo—a big, ugly, hairy, smelly *stud* buffalo. Some folks around these parts aren't too thrilled about her messing with new breeds, which might be why he's missing in the first place. Or maybe someone's trying to drive her out of business to buy the ranch. Who knows."

Maggie eyed Roy. "Andy is *not* ugly."

Jack's mouth opened and closed, but nothing came out. Finally, he managed to say, "All this is over a *buffalo?*"

"Technically, Andy's a bison."

He gave her the official Chicago-cop stare, the one guaranteed to put him in charge of any situation…except this wasn't Chicago. "Cattle rustling's dangerous." His comment failed to impress, and his stare slipped a notch. "Least, that's what I've heard."

Maggie's brow furrowed. "I don't believe it. You're in town what, ten minutes, and I'm getting a lecture on *danger* from Mr. Supercop? The guy who, for the past twenty years, has taken every hair-raising job in the Chicago police department that's come along."

She started counting on her fingers. "Let's see. There's been SWAT, undercover, riot control, counterterrorism, drug trafficking, organized crime, and only heaven can imagine what else. And taking one bull isn't cattle rustling so much as cattle *meddling.*"

He narrowed his eyes. "Roy can get someone else."

"*My* ranch and *my* buffalo." She stepped toward her handsome ex-husband. 'Course, he was also interfering, overwhelming, controlling, not happy unless surrounded by chaos and mayhem and more than a tad chauvinistic, all of which made him her *ex*.

She added, "I know about bison. It's my business and I'm taking it in a new direction. If I don't, Sky Notch will get gobbled up by the big conglomerates because we're a small ranch and can't compete in the cattle industry unless we find a niche. Andy's our niche."

"Damn, Maggie. You don't even own a gun. Do you?"

"We're not hunting drug dealers, Jack. My guess is some rancher wants to warn me off from trying something different, thinking the old way of ranching is the best. He's probably afraid Andy will spread disease or vermin or whatever, when just the opposite is true. He'll 'borrow' my cows and calves next. Tonight's a full moon, a perfect time to go after my cattle and for me to catch the guy red-handed." She glanced at Roy. "Are you in or out?"

He ran his hand over his face. "I'll see you tonight at eight."

She grinned, then headed out the door. Jack followed. "What's going on?" he asked. "You didn't do things like this in Chicago. You did volunteer work and put together those cute little scrapbooks about Ben growing up and—"

"And worried myself blue about you." She stopped on the sidewalk, nearly colliding with him as he followed. "I'm a different person, Jack. I *had* to change or lose everything. Ranching's different these days. But you're no different at all." Not the way he looked, not the way he behaved, not the way he affected her heartbeat and blood pressure even after all this time.

A cool spring breeze, mixed with the promise of summer heat, skimmed down the street, ruffling Jack's hair, making her remember when she'd done the ruffling. "Why *are* you here?"

His left eyebrow rose a fraction. "You invited me? Little blue card with the mortarboard on front, confetti inside that fell all over the damn place when I opened it? Sound familiar?"

She peered at him. "What happened? You're never early for anything. Dinner, movies, birth of your offspring."

He spread his hands wide, giving her the innocent look. It had to be a doozie to get the innocent look. She said, "You're limping."

"I tripped."

"Getting to what? Because I know that's not the end of the story. Jack Dawson doesn't trip unless he's going *into* a place everyone else is running *out* of."

"Well, there were these wires…blue and white…and they were sort of attached to an explosive device on the forty-eighth floor of the First National—"

"I knew it!" She clenched and unclenched her hands as old fears came thundering back like a stampede of wild horses. "And you're having a conniption over *me* finding a bull? You dismantle bombs, for God's sake."

"Not by choice."

Jack continued. "I just went into the bank to check on a college loan for Ben, then all hell broke loose, and there I was and the bomb squad wasn't, and what was I going to do?"

"So you wound up in the middle of it."

He gave her a lopsided grin that made her feel good all over because he was here and smiling at her like old times, the good old times, not the bad old times. How could that happen, when she wanted to wring his neck for nearly getting himself killed...*again?*

"I was an innocent bystander, and since I lucked out, I thought I'd come and hang with Ben and—"

"Maggie. Oh, Maggie," called a familiar voice from across the street as best friends one and two, Dixie and BJ, hurried her way. They flashed her a *gotcha* look as they drew up beside Jack, Dixie making dreamy eyes he couldn't see but Maggie could.

"Who is *this?*" Dixie cooed as she hooked her arm through Jack's.

Maggie cringed. She and Jack were about to get put in the hot seat and there wasn't one thing she could do to stop it. She said, "You both know darn well who this is. Thirteen years ago isn't that long."

BJ gave Jack the once-over. "Why, it's that cute cop whose picture's hanging on your wall. Imagine that." She stuck out her hand. "Nice seeing you, Jack Dawson. I'm BJ in case you forgot. Town doctor, buttinski friend."

Jack peered at Maggie. "You have my picture on your wall?"

"A little one. Behind a door."

Jack shook BJ's hand as Dixie said, "And I'm Dixie, the gorgeous buttinski friend and waitress at the Purple Sage. If you want to know what's going on in this town, just ask me." She fluffed her hair and batted her eyes.

"We didn't expect you for two more days, but welcome back to Whistlers Bend."

Jack arched his brow. *"We?"*

Dixie laughed. "Everybody knows when a hunky Chicago policeman who was once married to one of our own is headed this way. Heard you got shot in the rump last year. Bet that hurt." She pointed over her shoulder to Jack's back. "I noticed everything healed up real nice."

His eyes bulged. Small-town gossip could do that to an outsider, even a Chicago cop. He said, "It was just a flesh wound, and how'd you find out?"

Maggie said, "Your dad called. Henry thinks you're Wyatt Earp and Double-O-Seven all rolled into one. He brags about you every chance he gets, though getting shot in the backside doesn't exactly fit into the gossip category."

BJ shrugged. "Guess he thought it was local color."

Jack groused. "Isn't that like cookie recipes, cattle drives and new trucks?"

Dixie winked. "None of which holds a candle to *your*…butt." She giggled. "Oops. That could cause another flesh wound."

BJ said, "Don't mind Dixie. She flirts with every guy she meets, even your dad. No male escapes."

Maggie felt her eyes widen by half as BJ rushed on. "We ran into your folks over at Horn to Hoof. Terrific people. They took our picture. Said they'd meet up with you two later since you appeared to be having a nice conversation and they didn't want to interrupt."

Maggie's eyes pulled together. *"Folks?"*

Dixie said, "We're heading for the Sage. My shift is about to start. See you later. Don't hurry on our account. Enjoy yourself."

"Folks!"

Dixie patted Jack's cheek. "I'm sure we'll meet up again, Jack Dawson. You're all Maggie's talked about for months and months and months, and you're every bit as handsome and intriguing as she said."

Maggie folded her arms as Dixie and BJ left. "I never said any of those things. And would you care to tell me more about your parents being here."

"They're shopping for cowboy hats. Mom told Ben we were all coming in today, but obviously he never told you."

Maggie did an eye roll. "Big surprise there. And I had no idea your parents had such an affinity for the West. Where'd that come from?"

"A digital camera and too many John Wayne movies."

She gave her full attention to Jack, still not quite believing he was here in Whistlers Bend. She didn't understand the camera and hat references at all, but she'd get to that later when things weren't so hectic—like maybe when she turned ninety. "I really need to shop for groceries. After you find Gert and Edward, you can go on to the ranch." She pointed to the street. "Take this road and bear left. Dad may or may not be home. Tuesday's square-dancing day over at Rocky Fork. He never misses a square dance."

"If Henry's doing all this dancing, who's running the ranch?"

"The same person who's chasing after a buffalo. Whistlers Bend is a quiet, peaceful place, Jack. Please, please don't go stirring things up, okay?"

He gave her a *who-me?* look.

"You arrested two con men on our honeymoon. Right there in the middle of the Aladdin Hotel. The whole reason we went to Vegas in the first place to get married was to get you away from work and be totally alone together. While you're here, try real hard to forget you're a cop. Think *tourist.* Kick back and relax. Whittle."

Jack folded his arms across his solid chest. "I get to leave running after the bad guys to you."

"You're blowing that way out of proportion. This is not Dodge City at the turn of the century. I'm riding out with Roy to check on the cattle."

Jack nodded slowly. "Right. I won't get in your way." He smiled, and a spark lit his big brown eyes.

Her heart skipped a beat at the smile and her brain screamed *uh-oh* at the spark. "I mean it, Jack."

"Hey, so do I."

Right! Like she didn't have enough on her plate with Ben, Henry and Andy to deal with. And now Jack. All males. There was a message here. Weren't things supposed to be easier at forty? Level out? Get less complicated because kids had grown and relationships had settled? She had serious reservations about Ben maturing, and her relationship with Jack would never fit into the *settled* category. But, somehow, they were all family. "Ben will be thrilled you're here. And I do appreciate you coming *and* bringing your parents."

She took his hand, loving the feel of him more than she expected. Sure, strong, dependable. "You've always been a good son, helping your folks whenever they needed it, and a good father, being with Ben whenever you could."

"Just not much of a husband?"

She sighed. "It's an *us* thing. We're not a good couple, Jack. It took me a long time to figure out that sometimes love isn't enough. Our lives never meshed, no matter how hard we tried. It wasn't just your job. I never fit in Chicago."

She pulled in a breath and went on, trying to clear things between them. "School there was okay—I liked being a graphic artist. But living in Chicago, with all that concrete, crime and commotion, was another matter. And heaven knows an adrenaline junkie like you could never stay in Whistlers Bend. You'd die of boredom. I'm not sure what you're going to do for the next nine days."

She pressed a soft kiss to his cheek. An affectionate gesture to tell him she didn't blame him or herself that some relationships weren't meant to be. At least, that was the idea until a warm sensation flowed through her, like drinking hot chocolate on a cold Montana night.

She quickly stepped away. "But that's all behind us." She gave him a bright smile to hide her uneasy feeling. "We're older now, mature adults who see things more clearly and understand where we belong. We've moved on from trying to make things work between us when that was impossible. We're both happy with our choices. Right?"

"Absolutely."

"We got that straight. I feel better." She gave him a narrow-eyed look. "Do you feel better?"

"Great." He smiled at her and offered her a little two-fingered salute, just the way he'd done every morning when he'd gone off to work. He headed across the street.

She aimed for the Purple Sage. They agreed that nothing between them had changed because Jack had come to Whistlers Bend. She had her life here, and in nine days he'd go back to his life in Chicago. Ben's graduation represented a simple family get-together—short, sweet, uncomplicated. Nothing more.

She needed to remember that.

Chapter Two

Maggie walked under the striped awning of the Purple Sage Café and pushed open the door, which was framed with eyelet curtains. This time of day most booths and tables sat empty, awaiting the onslaught of the dinner crowd. The clatter of dishes and the aroma of cooking emanating from the kitchen gave the café a cozy, peaceful quality. She ignored the chocolate pie perched under the glass dome on the counter and made her way to the table by the front window.

She collapsed into the chair as BJ slid a cup of amaretto coffee toward her and said, "Dixie's warmed this three times in the microwave. It's got to taste like dead skunk by now. Mrs. Garvey cornered me and I got to hear about her gallbladder attack *again* and I have office hours in a half hour. It's nearly three. What took you so long to get here?" She wiggled her brows and grinned. "My bet's on a certain Chicago cop. And if that's the case, I don't mind waiting one bit."

"The Chicago cop's wandering around town, searching for his parents, who are off taking pictures and probably hoping for a stagecoach to rumble by. They're really into this Old West thing."

Dixie served her a toasted peanut-butter sandwich with a banana sliced on top. Maggie bit into it, careful not to lose any bananas as Dixie plucked at the collar of Maggie's blouse, her mouth twisting as if she'd swallowed a fly. "Well, if they're wanting the Old West, this faded blue blouse and your old denim skirt fit right in. They should be pleased as punch with Annie Oakley as an ex-daughter-in-law."

Maggie peered at her skirt. "What's wrong with my clothes? I always wear these clothes. Denim wears well and I happen to like Annie Oakley."

BJ brushed a nonexistent piece of lint from her perfect taupe silk blouse. "The original fashion diva of Whistlers Bend."

Maggie wagged her finger. "I know what you're up to. I wasn't born yesterday. You think I'm going to fall for Jack again. And if I look less like Annie Oakley and more like Meg Ryan he'll fall for me again, too, and we'll live happily every after."

Dixie faced BJ. "Where does she get ideas like that?"

Maggie snagged a banana slice and shook it at them. "Well, it's not going to happen. I'll never be Meg Ryan. She's blond—I'm brunette. She's size four—I'm a fourteen. Besides, I've got enough on my mind right now and I don't have time to shop, and if you think I'm going to make the time because Jack Dawson suddenly lands on my doorstep you're dead wrong." She ate the banana. "There's nothing, not one darn thing, between us except Ben."

BJ and Dixie exchanged looks and BJ said, "Do you remember saying anything about Jack? I don't remember saying anything about Jack. We were talking about the in-laws."

"And Annie Oakley." Dixie nodded vigorously and pointed to Maggie. "*She's* the one who brought up Jack. But now that she has…" Dixie patted Maggie on the head. "I'm sure he likes you just the forty-year-old way you are."

Maggie held out her hands, palms up. "I just turned forty last week, so I don't really have a *way,* and I don't care if Jack Dawson likes it or not."

Dixie nodded in agreement. "That's a good attitude to have and I bet Mary Lou Armstrong appreciates it, too."

Maggie took a bite of sandwich and swallowed. "What's Mary Lou got to do with this?"

"Nothing, except she's making goo-goo eyes at Jack in the middle of the street as we speak." Dixie hitched her chin at the window behind Maggie. "Didn't she just get divorced last month? And she's only thirty-five. Guess she decided to dye her hair platinum-blond and wear stiletto heels and that short pink skirt to give herself a little pick-me-up. I wonder who else she's going to *pick up.*"

Maggie didn't want to look, but something made her twist in her seat to face the window. Her jaw clenched as Jack smiled and laughed and seemed way too happy about talking to Mary Lou and her exposed cleavage. "He's supposed to be on his way to the ranch for pot roast."

Dixie tsked. "I think he's checking out dessert."

BJ added, "Maybe Mary Lou's giving him some directions."

Maggie hissed, "She's giving him *direction,* all right."

Dixie let out a sigh. "You can't blame the girl. Jack's forty, the older man, experienced, a real hunk." She fanned herself with a napkin. "He's hot in any gal's book."

Maggie snapped the napkin from Dixie as they turned back to the table. "He's forty-one and no one's baby, not that it matters to me. Mary Lou can skip that chapter of the book since the experienced *hunk* will be gone in nine days."

BJ smiled sweetly and said in a singsong voice, "But he's here now and he's mighty fine, indeed."

Maggie closed her eyes for a moment, collecting her thoughts and refusing to get all excited over Jack, because that was exactly what BJ and Dixie wanted so they could convince her she still had romantic feelings for him—*which she didn't.* She folded her hands on the table and squared her shoulders. "I will explain to you the way things are between me and Jack, and then we don't have to talk about him anymore. We are happy with our lives just as they are, and if he wants directions or dessert from Mary Lou, that's his affair, not mine."

"Did you say *affair?*" BJ asked.

Maggie gritted her teeth, keeping control. "I mean, *his business.*"

"But what about Ben's graduation?"

Maggie said, "How'd graduation get into this?"

Dixie continued, "Well, your whole family's here and you want to look nice for Ben's graduation."

"I have a suit."

"When Sean graduated last year I wore a dress I got at Saks, with matching Prada shoes and purse. Not that anyone noticed, since my dearly beloved ex brought his Barbie-doll, cleavage-enhanced new wife, who wore a napkin. Did I happen to mention she was a Victoria's Secret model and is closer to Sean's age than her husband's? Ever notice how models *never* smile. Think she has teeth?"

BJ shrugged. "Danny married her for her teeth, and at least you and Maggie have an ex and didn't get left standing at the altar with the whole town to witness it."

Dixie huffed. "Everyone in town knows Randall Cramer is a cheat, a con artist and a champion donkey's butt who's presently serving five-to-ten in the big house." She winked at BJ. "But you did look superb."

"Thank you." BJ nudged Maggie. "Imagine khaki, teal, green. Silk, satin, linen, lace. Do it for Ben. Pretty in Pink just got in a new shipment of summer fashions. Exercise that credit card, cowgirl. It's your duty as an all-American woman to support the economy. *Shop.*"

"I hate to shop. I don't have time to shop. My buffalo's missing and I have in-laws and an ex to contend with. My suit will do. This is yet another ploy to get me spruced up for Jack."

"The suit's gray and ugly. *Shop.*" Dixie fluffed her bob. "I would. I'm going red when I turn forty in two months. That gives me two months to decide." She gave BJ a superior smirk. "You have only *one* month left."

Dixie continued. "Maybe I'll get skinny. Go on one of those meat diets. Got to be better than the cabbage-soup diet. My house still reeks."

BJ drummed her fingers on the table. "That means you're abstaining from pizza and beer?"

Dixie frowned. "Pizza and beer contain all the food groups."

"And enough fat and carbs to kill a bear," BJ countered.

Maggie stood and said, "I dropped off a grocery list at the Daily Market. They'll have my order ready by now and I've got a houseful of people to feed. I'll get a new dress just to keep you both from hounding me."

Dixie placed her hands on her well-rounded hips. "We did a lot more hounding than one lousy dress's worth."

"Amen to that." Maggie glanced out the window. Mary Lou and Jack had gone. *Together?* Not that she cared. She hadn't cared for a long time what Jack did—well, pretty much—and she sure didn't care now.

JACK PACED the front porch of the ranch house, wondering where Maggie was at six o'clock. He also wondered what the hell had possessed her to go out searching for a stupid bull. Andy—what kind of name was that for a bison?

It was dangerous, dammit. And the sheriff's job. Why didn't she get that? Someone who stole something valuable had no intention of handing it over without a fight.

What if Roy couldn't protect her? How could this happen in a little town in Montana? Hadn't Wild West stuff like this ended a long time ago?

Right. Just the way armed robbery in the city had ended a long time ago. Crime went on forever.

He paced again, slower this time, favoring his bad leg. He took in the rustic setting. What a contrast to his apartment back in Chicago and his parents' place in the burbs. Sky Notch. The name fit. The ranch seemed as much part of the heavens as it did earth.

He studied the floorboards. Logs, real ones, and a huge rock chimney. A gravel driveway circled in front. Pine trees, thick grass and boulders were everywhere. Barns stood off to one side, with cattle here and there, but no buffalo. Would he even know a buffalo if he saw one? The only thing buffalo he'd ever dealt with was buffalo *wings.*

He sat down on the rocking chair, rocked two times—and spied a thick trail of dust heading his way. When the Suburban stopped beside his rental van, it coughed, backfired twice, shuddered, then died in a cloud of blue exhaust.

Who was that getting out of the— *"Maggie?"* He hopped down the the steps and looked her over, head to toe. "You cut your hair. A lot. Where are your clothes? *Your curls?* What have you done?"

She pulled packages from the back seat. "My clothes are on, Jack. Least, I hope so, since they cost the earth. The curls are in a trash can at the Curly Cactus." She nudged the car door shut with a hip as he scrambled down the steps to help her. "I needed a dress for Ben's graduation and picked up a few other things. I ran late so I just kept this on. Where are your parents?"

He paused for a moment, taking in some spicy scent she'd never worn before, as far as he knew. Her haircut exposed the back of her neck, her lovely delicate neck. Her eyes seemed bluer, her face radiant. Her lips sensual, full, tempting. *Ah, hell.*

He nodded toward the barns. "The Lone Ranger and Tonto are taking their new Stetsons for a spin and riding the range with one of your hands."

He'd liked the Maggie he'd seen in town just fine, but *this* Maggie…his insides hummed…the new improved version? Damn! Why couldn't she wait till he'd left to get improved?

None of this mattered. Maggie was his ex. *Remember that. Ex! Ex! Ex!* "You look…nice."

She smiled and handed him the bags, then followed him onto the porch.

That smile. Maggie's smile. How many times had he come through the door of their apartment to that smile and everything in the world had suddenly seemed right and good again? Considering he dealt with the underbelly of Chicago day after day, that was going some.

"Why didn't you wait inside?" she asked as she toed the small mound of luggage, bringing him back to the moment.

He nodded at the door. "I didn't have a key and B and E is against the law."

She crossed the porch and turned the knob. "No need

for breaking and entering. If anyone wants to B and E around here there's no one to stop them."

The door swung open and he shook his head in wonder. "Incredible. Not locked. Who would have thought. Welcome to the boonies."

"Some of us call it home." And it was, for Maggie. She belonged here with the clear sky, mountains and pine trees as a backdrop, as much as the Sears Tower, Navy Pier and smog belonged in his life.

She reached for a suitcase, but he put the packages in one hand and beat her to it, her fingers closing over his. Her touch felt intimate. His pulse pounded. He didn't want intimate. He sure as heck didn't want her new perfume driving him nuts. He thought of her life, then his, and how they were more different than ever. He didn't need to get wrapped up in Maggie Moran's new look or her old familiar touch only to leave them behind in nine days. He was the master of cool and neutral, everyone at the precinct said so. *Remember that!* he admonished himself.

Instead, he remembered the time he was in the hospital recovering from gunshot wounds. He'd dreamed Maggie was there with him, touching him, making him feel loved and cared for. Remembering *that* plus getting bombarded in the past five minutes with all her other attributes shot cool and neutral to hell and back. His reaction to Maggie got way more *physical* than he expected.

Great, now what? How long could he stay hunched over his own luggage? He wasn't some horny teen. He was a mature adult, in control of his life. *This* should not happen.

Maggie scowled as she righted herself. "Couldn't you just leave that *thing* in Chicago?"

He gulped. "*Leave…it?*"

"You won't need that nine-millimeter something-or-other in your pocket. Put your gun somewhere else till you go. People in Whistlers Bend don't pack *heat,* unless you count a cigarette lighter."

He thought of his Glock at his apartment, locked in a box in his closet. Now wasn't the first time his gun had saved him, but never quite like *this.* "Ah, sure, I can do that. No guns." *He hoped.*

He had known he'd be attracted to Maggie when he got here, but as Ben's middle-aged mom. Well, guess what, Skippy! Maggie was a lot more than Ben's mom, and middle age was a damn good age, at least on her.

A red car tore up the gravel driveway, spewing stones and dust everywhere and taking the focus off him for the moment. Thank heaven for the diversion. He stood, directing her attention to the car. "Is that Ben? He knows better than to drive like that." Jack glanced at Maggie. "Doesn't he?"

Maggie folded her arms and groused, "Oh, yes. Ben knows better, but that's *not* Ben."

The red Mustang slid to a spitting stop. "*Jack?*" came a man's voice from inside. "What in blue blazes are you doing here? Weren't expecting you for two days."

Jack blinked and dropped his bag back on the porch,

remembering to put Maggie's packages down with a bit more care. "Mr. Moran?"

He laughed as he slid from the car. "What's with this mister stuff? What happened to *Dad?*"

The men shook hands and bear-hugged as Maggie glared at her father. "Where were you last night? Why didn't you call? I worried and worried. You are so… so…so *grounded.*"

Her dad laughed again and draped his big arm around her shoulders, drawing her near and kissing her on the cheek. "What's for dinner? I'm famished." He turned to Jack. "Sure is good to lay eyes on you again. How are things in Chicago?"

"Not quite as booming as they could be. Nice set of wheels."

"Yep, she's a honey, all right." Henry swiped his hand over the smooth finish. "After the heart attack I gave my pickup to Ben and bought myself the Mustang. She was a wreck, but I fixed her up. Four-on-the-floor, custom red metallic paint, surround sound, the whole enchilada."

Maggie stepped out of her father's embrace. "So, where were you all night and all the rest of today? You're making me nuts."

"Do I ask you that when you go out riding half the night? Hey—what did you do to your hair and clothes?" He winked. "Got yourself all gussied up for Jack, huh?"

She huffed. "When I go out at night I'm looking for Andy. Our beefalo herd won't get any larger if the dear boy isn't here to sow his wild oats, and I am not *gussied.*"

Jack asked, "What kind of herd?"

The warm breeze tossed Maggie's hair into a frenzy and she smoothed it back. He stuffed his hands into his pockets to keep from touching it as she said, "Beefalo, a cross between bison and beef cattle. Less fatty meat, range-fed, no hormone-growing agents, disease resistant, a good market for a smaller ranch." Her face crinkled with a half smile. "I sound like an advertisement. But they're as cute as the devil. Buffalo roamed these plains long before cattle, so they're well suited to the area." She shrugged. "*Beefalo*. At least, if I find Andy I'll have beefalo."

Jack gave Henry a man-to-man look. "Talk her out of this. It's a bad idea."

Henry held up his hands in surrender. "I've tried. In fact, I think we should sell the ranch and move to town. Big ranches are the only ones making a real profit these days. This beefalo thing is real chancy, if you ask me."

Jack rested his hand on Henry's shoulder and peered at him. "I mean, talk her out of going after Andy."

Maggie's brow furrowed. "No one's going to talk me out of anything and we're not selling and moving to town. This is our home. Always has been, always will be."

Laughing, Henry slapped Jack on the back. "I'll be leaving now. I got my hands full, keeping Irene in line. That's where I was last night. Over in Rocky Fork. Irene's my partner and we were practicing for the square-dance competition in Butte next month. Doing a little do-si-do."

He winked at Jack. "Just kidding. Irene would have my scalp if she heard me talking cheeky like that. Kind of nice to tease her once in a while, though. Keeps the blood flowing. Anyway, we really were practicing and I slept on her couch 'cause it got late and I forgot to call." He cupped Maggie's chin in his hand. "Sorry about that."

Jack did a mental head shake. At the moment, he found it hard to tell who was the parent and who was the child. For sure, Maggie ran the ranch and Henry ran the Mustang. After all the years of ranching, he was entitled, but that was a hell of a lot of responsibility for his daughter. The rancher's daughter was now the rancher.

Maggie nodded at Henry. "Just call next time. You could have been—"

"Dead by the side of the road. You've told me before. But that's not going to happen for a long time." He puffed out his chest and grinned. "I feel better than ever. What's for dinner? Roast, butter rolls, chocolate cake?"

"For you, vegetable soup, fruit salad, vanilla yogurt."

"How's a man supposed to live on soggy vegetables and slimy milk?" He pulled at the red-and-yellow Hawaiian-print shirt he wore and nodded at Jack. "Picked this up in town. Just got them in. Snazzy huh? Goes with the car."

Henry made for the steps until a *yee-haa* came from the barns and Gert, Edward and Lucky rounded the corner on horseback, Gert and Edward waving their hats in the air.

"Well, tie me up and brand me." Henry nodded at Jack. "Your parents? Hot-diggity-dog. Didn't think they were coming in until next week. We'll paint the town red tonight."

Henry took off in a fast walk, waving back as Jack was saying to Maggie, "Why didn't you call me when your dad had a heart attack?"

"I did. You were undercover. It was for the best. You would have come running, taken charge like you always do and made the hospital staff and me loony."

He leaned against one of the cedar posts of the porch. "I don't always take charge. I can do laid-back."

She gave him a wide-eyed look that said *Wanna bet.*

He shrugged. "All right, I suck at laid-back. I wish I could have been here for you."

"Dad's fine now, but he's not up to running the ranch anymore."

"So now it's up to you?"

"That or lose the place. Let's eat. Then you and Dad and your folks can watch Ben's baseball game. He'll be thrilled to see you."

The breeze caught her green silky blouse, molding it to her full breasts. A mature woman's shape…one he'd like to get his hands on. *Bad idea!* "What about you? Aren't you coming?"

She turned for the door. "I have a date with a deputy."

Date? Even though she didn't mean it as a date kind of date he didn't like the sound of it. "I can do backup. I'm great at backup. Do it much better than laid-back. And I can ride a horse. If Gert and Edward can ride, I sure can."

She paused with her hand on the doorknob. "Spending a half hour in a saddle is not like spending four hours. You wouldn't be able to sit for days."

"When I got shot in the ass I couldn't sit for longer than that. I'll survive."

She reached up and tweaked his chin, the old familiar gesture catching him off guard. And for a second it seemed to have the same effect on her. Neither said anything for a beat, the whole world suddenly still. Her eyes got a little smoky. "You'll enjoy the game. Ben's a great shortstop. Wish some of that greatness carried over to chemistry."

She opened the door. "Take a break from being a cop, Jack. With a little luck, whoever has Andy will return tonight and we'll straighten this mess out."

"What if they try to straighten it out with a shotgun?" He put her packages on the table in the hallway, the same table that had been there years ago, the same baby picture of Ben in the same silver frame. As she helped him move the luggage inside by the steps, he said, "Let your workers do it. That Lucky guy is capable."

She closed the door. "He and two others are riding out to some of the pastures and checking them. Roy and I will handle the others. I'm in good hands. Roy's a good deputy. Don't worry."

Dang! Wasn't that his line? At least, it had been thirteen years ago, when *he'd* gone off to work and *she'd* stayed home and he'd told *her* not to worry. How did life get flipped upside down like this?

By MIDNIGHT, as Jack paced the living room, he didn't have the answer, only another question: where the hell was Maggie? He climbed the steps two at a time to Ben's room, knocked, then went inside.

Ben turned from his computer. "What's up, Dad?"

Jack paced around a pile of jeans and T-shirts on the floor, stepped over in-line skates, dodged two bats and a well-worn glove. "You played a really good game today."

Ben grinned and leaned back in his chair. "Thanks again."

Jack looked to Ben. "I said that before, didn't I?"

"Three times on the ride home. I *am* going to graduate, if that's what's bothering you. I'm finishing up my very last chemistry lab report right now. I hate science. Guess that's why I've decided to be a business major, *if* I can get into college. I'm on the waiting list."

Jack paced back the other way, getting better at traversing the obstacles and resisting the urge to wring his son's neck for not keeping up his grades. "I wish your girlfriend could have been at the game. I'd like to meet her."

Ben shook his head. "I'll bring her around sometime. What's going on with you?"

"With me?" Jack stopped and faced Ben. He needed a haircut before graduation. What kid didn't? Jack spied his old SWAT jacket, which he'd given to Ben, hanging over the bedpost, and a picture of himself and Ben at about four years of age, the boy wearing Jack's policeman's hat. He remembered when Maggie had taken that picture down by Navy Pier at the Ferris wheel. "What kind of deputy is Roy?"

"Mr. Hanson?" Ben shrugged his young broad shoulders. "Fine, I guess. He's fair, doesn't take any grief from the kids. Mom likes him."

Jack's chest felt tight. She liked him. What did that mean?

"He and your mother have been gone for nearly four hours." *In the dark, alone,* he added to himself. Jack gazed out Ben's bedroom window, which faced the front yard. "Do you think they're okay? If this was Chicago I could have the black-and-whites watch out for her car, but—"

"Well, this isn't Chicago and she's not in a car." Ben chuckled, stood and put his hand on Jack's shoulder. "Mom's fine. She's tough, Dad. Nothing gets by her. She's searching for Andy. She'll be back soon."

The clock on Ben's nightstand flashed red numbers, clicking off the minutes. Jack remembered the bomb at the First National. What was worse—that or Maggie riding the range at night? He'd had some control over the bomb. More than he had over Maggie? Hell, with her all he could do was sit around and wait on the sidelines.

Again he peered out the window. "I'm not much good at waiting."

Ben arched his eyebrows. "Really? I hadn't noticed."

"Smart-ass kid." Jack chuckled.

"We can play some computer games if you want."

Jack turned from the window. "So you can beat me black-and-blue?"

Ben laughed. "Just a little."

The clip-clop of hooves crunching gravel broke the stillness.

"That's Mom and Roy now, not the hands. I recognize her laugh."

So did Jack. And just what the devil was so funny at midnight—make that ten minutes after midnight? "Maybe I should go see if I can help her unsaddle the horse or something."

Ben's brown eyes grew wide. "Sweet. You know how to unsaddle a horse?"

Jack raked a hand through his hair. "Not really, but I'll figure it out." He patted Ben on the back. "You really *did* play one heck of a game. I mean it, Ben." He grinned. "I'm glad I was here for it."

"Me, too. Now, you better go help Mom and I better finish this report, or you'll have come fifteen-hundred miles for nothing."

"Hey, I've gotten to see you. That's all I want." Jack mussed his son's hair and nodded at the computer screen. "Waited till the last minute?"

Ben chuckled. "Would I do that?"

Jack yanked open the bedroom door, which had a picture of Brittany Spears on the back, and raced outside and down the steps, not caring squat that he didn't have on shoes…until he hit the gravel driveway. *Oh, hell.* Shoes would be good here. But he wasn't about to go back. Besides, he'd lost his shoes, since he'd been pacing in bare feet half the night. One thing he did realize—this Andy thing had gone on long enough.

He waited a few moments and watched Roy's truck

and horse trailer drive off, then he made his way across the pebbles toward the barn door, lit by a dim overhead bulb. He finally caught up with Maggie, who was leading her horse in that direction. "'Bout damn time you got home."

Gads, he sounded like a fishwife. Right now he felt like one. He didn't care.

"Jack?" She faced him, her skin almost translucent in the faint light. "You scared the life out of me. I didn't hear you coming and—" She eyed his feet. "Lose something?"

Stars dotted the sky. A cool breeze rolled across the yard, carrying the scent of fresh earth and spring grass. Cows mooed. A rabbit darted behind the house. They were surrounded by a sense of space and timelessness that had never existed in Chicago—least in the past two hundred years. "It's after midnight."

"Meaning?" She gave him a questioning look.

"You've been out there—" he pointed into the darkness "—for over four hours, searching for a buffalo."

"And had no luck at all. Are the parents home?"

"Painted the town in two hours flat and now they're sawing logs. What if you met up with those rustlers? What were you going to do? Talk them into giving Andy back and send them home with a warning not to do it again?"

"Yes."

If she'd slapped him upside the head with a sack of pine cones he couldn't have been more surprised. "You're serious?"

She drew her jacket closer against the night chill. "Someone's trying to ruin Sky Notch. Roy and I need to figure out who it is and why they're doing this and then talk them out of it. This is not a range war. No one else is involved. It's just Sky Notch."

"You and old Roy are an item, is that it?" A fire ignited in his gut, but he tamped it down and forced a smile. He had no claim on Maggie. So why the hell did he feel as if he did?

Her mouth pulled tight. He'd liked it better this afternoon all pink and lush. "Not that it's any of your business, but Roy is happily married, with four kids, two dogs and a gerbil named Godzilla, and I've known his wife and him since grade school. He and I used to fight like brother and sister because he was a big tease. And why do you care who I'm with, anyway?"

Damn good question. He let out a long breath while rubbing his neck. "Ben would be devastated if anything happened to you."

She folded her arms, her eyes big and blue, even in the faint light. "I've cared for myself and Ben for a long time, Jack. Then Dad had the heart attack and I tended to him and minded the ranch. I had no idea we were in such bad shape financially and it's up to me to do something, or Sky Notch is gone. This is my home. Andy is only a small part of my problems and you're worrying about me for nothing. I'm fine. I've made it this far. The beefalo idea is going to work."

She straightened his collar and offered him a disarming smile, except he was a Chicago cop and not easily disarmed.

She added, "You deserve a break, a real vacation.

Think of something to do that's fun. Yellowstone Park's near. Plan a hike. Visit Old Faithful and watch something blow up besides a bank."

"And you'll keep riding out to heaven knows where?"

"I know where. I live here." She stroked her horse and the animal nuzzled Maggie's shoulder. Big horse, brown, impatient.

"Someone's sure to spot a buffalo hanging around. Besides, this is Whistlers Bend. Nothing happens in Whistlers Bend that someone doesn't find out about sooner or later. Everyone's business is a way of life."

The horse nudged her again, and she stumbled into Jack. He caught her out of pure instinct—legs to legs, hips to hips, chest to breasts, her lips only a breath from his.

Damn.

He'd missed her. Maggie felt soft and warm and exciting against him. He regretted every disparaging remark he ever thought about horses. Cars couldn't make her stumble into him like this. And even though he shouldn't, he liked her there more than he thought possible. Yet, wasn't he supposed to be over her? Didn't attractions fade when people were separated over so many miles and so many years?

His gaze met hers, and for a moment they were together just as they had been that first magical year they were married, nothing keeping them apart. No problems, no worries, only love. Then she stepped back, taking the moment and the memories with her, leaving him alone.

He didn't appreciate how alone till he'd held her, then didn't.

She smoothed back her hair from her cheek. "You've had a long day. You need sleep."

"I can't sleep knowing you'll be right back out here tomorrow night, wandering all over the countryside."

She set her chin and pointed to the house. "I was born there, Jack, and my mother died there when I was five. It's my home. I'm not giving it up because some rancher doesn't want me to upset the cattle world, or whatever crazy reason he has. And if he thinks I'm an easy mark because I'm a forty-year-old woman, he'd better think again."

She led her horse into the barn, calling over her shoulder, "This isn't your business any more than being a cop in Chicago is mine."

Except this time *he* wasn't the one in danger; *she* was, on a little ranch in Montana. He had to protect her. He was a cop; that was what he did, whether in Chicago or anyplace else. He couldn't just stand by and do nothing for the next nine days. *That was for sure.*

Chapter Three

The noon sun blazed as Maggie drove into town the next day to help Roy with paperwork. Not her favorite pastime, but she'd promised. She parked the Suburban behind Henry's Mustang. What was he doing here? she wondered while waiting for the last belch of exhaust to clear before Big Blue died, hopefully not for good. Didn't the fearsome foursome have plans today?

She got out and spotted BJ, coughing and waving away residual smoke. "Now I need a lung transplant." She grinned. "Nice haircut and makeup…for Ben's graduation."

"Even an old barn deserves a coat of fresh paint once in a while."

"Doesn't sound like Christian Dior."

"Dolly Parton."

"So what was Jack Dawson's reaction to the new paint and do? Did he salivate? Tongue on the ground? Pant?"

"He said I looked nice."

BJ's eyes widened. "That's it?"

Maggie nodded. "See, I told you there was nothing

between Jack and me. The *nice* didn't even come with a raised brow or the obligatory wink. I've been reduced to *nice* status. We're history, *ancient* history."

If she really believed that, why had she thought about Jack all night? Why was she wearing makeup in case she ran in to him? Because being held in Jack Dawson's strong arms had done that to her. And for the first time in a really long time she felt like a woman, not chief, cook and the Donald Trump of Sky Notch.

BJ waved in Maggie's face, getting her attention. "Dreaming about Jack?"

"Analyzing him." Maggie started toward the sheriff's office and BJ fell into step beside her. "If he had his way I'd forget about Andy, sell Sky Notch and get a house in town."

"He doesn't know you at all."

"He thinks I'm the same woman who lived in Chicago thirteen years ago. It's best if Jack and I stay away from each other, if I keep him out of my life so he doesn't try to run it. That's exactly what he'll try to do."

"How do you know he hasn't changed?" BJ asked as she opened the door to the sheriff's office and Maggie followed her in. "He'd older, wiser and—"

"And he's sitting in the middle of the sheriff's office, behind the sheriff's desk," Maggie interrupted. "What are you doing here?"

"'Morning, Maggie," he said.

Her heart flipped. How many times had she heard those words when he'd come off a night shift after doing whatever hair-raising thing had crossed his path? How many times had she breathed a sigh of relief just seeing him alive, all body parts attached? "What happened to you? Gert and Edward going to Yellowstone? Where's the minivan? I didn't see the van."

Maggie glanced at Roy. Takeout from the Purple Sage cluttered his desk and Jack chomped a French fry, then said around a mouthful, "I'm not the Yellowstone type. Henry and Irene took my parents and the van. I borrowed Henry's Mustang. You were in the barn, talking to that guy who shoes the horses, when all this happened."

An uneasy feeling crept up her spine, and it wasn't about the smithy and the horses. "And you're here because…"

"Roy has a little problem. He's shorthanded."

"I know. I'm helping with paperwork."

"But what about the other work, the sheriff work?" Jack put down the fry and leaned forward, bracing his arms on the desktop. "I'm a cop and I can—"

"No!" Maggie felt her eyebrows shoot to her hairline. *"Absolutely not!* No way, Jack. You're not doing this. Forget it." She shook her head. "This is not happening in my own backyard. I left you and law enforcement and sleepless nights and nail-biting days in Chicago. You're not coming here and doing the very thing—"

"It's Whistlers Bend."

"I don't care if it's the moon."

"Nothing's going to happen. Roy just needs another hand and I'm here for eight more days. Ben's in school, the parents are doing the tourist thing, you have Andy and—"

"Aha!" She pointed an accusing finger at him. "That's it. This is all about you protecting me." She narrowed her eyes, hoping her brows followed and weren't permanently fixed to her hairline. "You'll go everywhere with me, offer sage advice and drive me totally bonkers. Blast your controlling hide, Jack Dawson." Although it was a very nice hide.

BJ stepped back. "I'll go now. You kids have fun."

Maggie gave her a slitty-eyed stare. "Coward."

"Oh, absolutely." BJ headed for the door and Roy stood. "Some of the seniors over at the high school are celebrating their graduation already and have skipped classes. Heard they were drag racing out at the old depot. I'll deal with them and leave you two to hash this out."

He nodded at Jack, then Maggie. "Leave the office intact—I have enough to deal with. Though another sheriff on board would—"

"Traitor," Maggie growled.

"I'm going, I'm going," Roy said, and held up his hands as if warding off a charging bull, then backed his way across the floor to the door and closed it quickly behind him.

Jack asked, "The old depot? What's that?"

"Old railroad station outside of town where the silver mine used to be. Engineers used to blow the whistle at the bend there to tell the miners the train was coming, and you're not changing the subject that easily."

"Think Ben's at the depot?"

His voice held a hint of parental worry. She understood all about being a parent and worry and how it sat in your stomach like a clump of underdone pasta until your son appeared in the doorway. Sympathy for Jack edged out her anger. "Not unless he wants to be grounded till he's thirty. And he had a chemistry lab report due. If he messes up that class, he's toast."

Jack leaned back in the chair, relief in his eyes. She knew that feeling, too. He gave her an easy smile.

"You are not charming your way out of this."

"I'm charming?" The smile grew; she steeled herself against it.

"Forget helping Roy."

Jack stood. Worn jeans. Blue chambray shirt with rolled-up sleeves, exposing muscled forearms sprinkled with dark hair. No trim, slim-hipped pretty boy here. Jack Dawson was made of sturdy stuff, inside and out. Solid, like Andy, and neither took grief from anyone.

He said, "Roy can go after Andy with you and without offering sage advice. I can hold down the fort here. I'll handle any disturbances that might come up in town, and—"

"You have no jurisdiction here."

His eyes didn't waver. "I'm qualified, trust me."

"You're a big-city policeman, Jack. You're aggressive and you'll scare the bejeebers out of everyone here. You don't know the people, what they're about, who does what. Like Jessica Banks, for instance. She works at Cellar to Ceiling Hardware till three and has to get her kids off the school bus at three-ten. You'd give her a speeding ticket when you saw her red truck fly through town, whereas the rest of us remember to stand back and let her go. Or Mr. Crawford. He shoplifts from the stores—can't help himself. The merchants just do a running tab and his son pays at the end of the month. What if you arrested him? You'd terrify the poor man to death."

He stared at her, then said, "This is for real?"

"No worse than any other town, but we help one another out and we all get along. We know which dogs can run loose and which ones need to be on a leash because they bite. Dixie's a waitress at the Purple Sage and remembers who gets rye and who gets whole wheat and who can't pay because they're out of a job and eats free till they find work. That's how small towns operate."

Her insides churned and she could barely breathe; she fought to keep her voice even. "You can't be sheriff. If you do I'll worry even if this is Whistlers Bend, where nothing ever happens. Me in a tizzy is a knee-jerk reaction to you and law enforcement, along with your uncanny ability to attract trouble wherever you go. For once in your life just do nothing."

"If I don't become sheriff you'll run after Andy alone and *I'll* worry."

"Okay. I can live with that. It's your turn. If you want something to do, take square dancing with Henry tomorrow. You might really like square dancing."

He gave her an icy Chicago-cop stare.

"Or not. *But you can't be sheriff.*"

JACK CLOSED the door to the sheriff's office behind him. *Well, hell! She'd kicked him out.* No one had kicked him

out of anywhere in a really long time, and the only reason Maggie had succeeded was that she had some very
valid points. As she'd rightly said, he didn't know the
town or the people, and he didn't want her to worry
about him being sheriff. She'd done that enough in
Chicago and he would not add to her worries now. But
he had to do something.

He crossed the street to the Sage. The purple-and-
white awning flapped in the breeze; purple-and-yellow
flowers bobbed in window boxes. If he ate he could figure out what to do. Coffee and pie would help. The best
brain food around. 'Course he would run a ton of miles
to burn off the calories.

When he entered the diner everyone stopped eating
and stared at him like the opening scene of some movie.
Uh-oh. Had he forgotten to put on his shoes again? He
looked down. Nope, shoes on, pants on, everything
zipped. Hell, he was in good shape. *What gives?*

"Howdy, handsome," Dixie greeted him. She hooked
her arm through his and escorted him to a table. "You
sure do a lot to brighten up this town—and Maggie."
She nodded at the customers, who still stared at him.
"And you give us all something to talk about besides the
weather and the price of beef."

"I do all that?"

She chuckled and took her pad from her purple apron
as he sat down. "BJ and I tried to convince that ex-wife
of yours to cut her hair for a year with no luck. Except
for running that ranch and Ben, she's on autopilot. You
show up and in one afternoon she cuts her hair and

buys a new wardrobe. Yeah, you brighten her up just dandy."

Dixie winked. "So, what's going on with you and Maggie, hmm?"

The old bait-and-switch routine. She'd given him some dirt; now she wanted some in return. Why not. He and Maggie weren't some big secret. Besides, with a diner full of eyes staring his way he couldn't conjure up a decent lie on the spot. "Nothing's going on. Hasn't been for a long time. I'm overbearing, controlling, work twenty-four/seven and love what I do. Maggie likes running the ranch and calling the shots there. But I wouldn't mind helping Roy, since he's shorthanded and all."

Had he just said "and all"?

A stocky woman in a business suit stood. "Seems to me that since you're Ben's daddy, you can start by helping your own son. You got the same problem as the rest of us. Graduation! God help us all."

Heads nodded in agreement as she continued. "Some seniors are causing bedlam already. Just think what graduation night's going to be like around here. My Barry graduates and I don't want anything to happen to him because he goes crazy for one night. But he turned eighteen and he sure as heck isn't listening to anything I'm saying these days."

Dixie brought Jack a piece of lemon meringue pie and coffee. Guess he looked like a man who needed pie and coffee.

Another waitress offered, "My Freddie graduates next year and I'm worrying myself to death already. Last year two cars full of kids were out joy-riding and had a terrible accident. Everyone's okay now, but they weren't then." Her voice caught and fear lined her face. "We need to do something. I just don't know what."

A man in a red plaid flannel shirt stood. He pushed his cowboy hat to the back of his head, swaggered and frowned, looking none too friendly. "If you want to help all of us, get your ex to give up this dang-fool beefalo idea. We don't want it and she's just stirring up problems. Can't she leave well enough alone? This is Montana. We raise cattle here. Real cattle, and we aren't much on changing our way."

Another man at the counter, in a leather vest, stood. "That's your opinion, Butch. Henry's a good man and fine rancher. We all respect him and now Maggie's carrying on."

"Maggie's not Henry," the plaid-shirt guy groused. "She has no idea what she's doing with that ranch. Beefalo? What the hell's that all about? Damn-fool idea. What about the disease that comes with buffalo? Ever think of that?"

The guy in the vest stepped toward Butch. "Same ones we get from deer, coyote and all the rest. You always were thickheaded about changing with the times."

The two men came nose-to-nose in the middle of the diner. Chicago or Montana, guys spoiling for a fight all looked alike—beady eyes, flared nostrils, red faces, fisted hands.

Butch glared. "Maggie's buffalo has run off and could be spreading God knows what to our cattle out on—"

"He didn't run off," interrupted the guy with the leather vest. "Bet you went and grabbed him. Maybe you're working with one of those conglomerates and forcing Maggie to sell. She's got a nice little spread there."

"You calling me a rustler, Pruitt?"

"If the shoe fits."

Butch threw a punch and Jack stood, snagging his coffee and pie from the table and backing up as the other guy sailed across it onto the floor. Jack took a drink of coffee. Should he break up the fight or not? He wasn't exactly one of the good old boys, and people here had their own way of doing things. Maggie had just lectured him on that very subject.

Pruitt stood, growled, dusted himself off and returned the punch as Maggie burst through the door yelling, "That's enough, you two."

Jack doubted that. When guys made up their minds to duke it out they weren't about to pay attention to a woman—no matter how good she smelled or how lovely she looked today—just because she was doing paperwork for Roy. *Damn, who called the sheriff's office?*

Pruitt threw another punch and Butch careened backward, crashing into Maggie and knocking her to the floor, her head hitting hard.

Jack dropped the pie and coffee on the nearest table with a clatter, snagged Pruitt with one hand and Butch with the other and held them apart. Jack put on his best, most threatening, don't-even-think-about-messing-with-me, Chicago-cop stare. "This fight is over!"

He shook the men like rag dolls. "Pay for the damages, get out and don't come back till Dixie says you can. Got it?"

Pruitt and Butch stared at Jack wide-eyed and nodded.

"Good. Now, get out and let folks eat in peace."

Butch snagged his hat from the floor and knocked the dust from it. Pruitt did the same. Jack grabbed Maggie under her arms and hauled her upright. He looked her in the eyes. "Dammit all! Are you okay?"

"Peachy."

He sat her in a chair and Dixie put a cup of tea in her hand. "Should we call BJ and have her make sure you're okay?"

Maggie blinked a few times. "I'm fine." She gave a big toothy grin and her eyes rolled round like marbles in an empty box.

Jack felt his gut tighten. Maggie, *his Maggie,* hurt on the floor. He was a cop; he protected people. The good citizens of Whistlers Bend would have to get used to the idea. "I'll take you home."

"Okeydoke."

Jack wondered where the heck that crack had come from, then added, "With a stop at BJ's on the way."

THE SUN HOVERED over the mountaintops, as if pausing before ending the day. Jack swung the saddle toward Butterfly, missed and called the four-legged critter that refused to stand still every name but *horse.* Henry laughed and leaned on the top rung of the corral. "You can't ride him if you can't saddle him. Sure you don't want me to lend a hand?"

Jack held up the saddle again and aimed for Butterfly's back—just as the horse backed away, leaving Jack
to saddle thin air. He wiped sweat from his forehead.
"He's laughing at me."

"It happens," Henry said with a laugh of his own.
"You got to make the horse understand who's boss, then
he'll stand still for you."

"I could read him his rights and lock him in jail."

"It's a pity Ben's not here to see this. He could razz
you for years to come."

Jack gave Butterfly his best threatening glare and
said to Henry, "Is he at practice?"

The horse grinned, Jack swore and Henry answered,
"He's got a date with *that girl.*"

Jack rested the saddle on the fence. His gaze met
Henry's. "Have you met her?"

"Nope. All I've heard is that she dropped out of
school and got picked up a few times for shoplifting
from Pretty in Pink. Maggie's not thrilled."

Jack exhaled, feeling his hair turn gray on the spot.
"Maybe I should have a talk with him."

"We've tried. He just gets all defensive and says we
got to trust him."

"Yeah, at eighteen he thinks he knows everything. By
forty-one he'll realize he doesn't know squat, especially
about women. I'll give Ben a few days of *trust,* then we
talk." Jack took up the saddle again, swung and missed
Butterfly for the millionth time.

He sighed and held out the saddle to Henry. "The

horse wins—I lose. He'll have to get saddled if I'm going with Maggie tonight and—"

"You're what?" Maggie asked as she rounded the corner of the corral. She stepped onto the bottom rung and peered over the top. Well-worn jeans, scuffed boots…this was not his Chicago Maggie; this was Montana Maggie, rancher, woman in charge. Wisps of red-and-gold hair peeking from under her hat caught the fading sunlight.

Damn, she was a beauty. He admired that, *and* he admired her hard work. When Henry had gotten sick, she could have packed it in, but she didn't. "Roy said you were heading out to look for Andy again. You shouldn't. You had a nasty hit."

"BJ said I was okay."

"She said you should take it easy."

"I rested for three hours. I'm all rested out."

Henry stretched. "You two can figure this out on your own. I've got a hot date with Irene tonight and I better not be late." He nodded to Jack. "We're taking your folks to a barn dance over in Stillwater. Your dad got a new western shirt with real pearl buttons and your mom got one of those full skirts with the petticoats underneath."

Jack winced. "*My* mom? *My* dad?"

Henry laughed. "Guess those Chicago roots don't run as deep as they thought. Montana affects people that way."

Henry walked toward the house and Jack put on his best smile for Maggie, the one he hoped made him look as though he knew what the hell he was doing when he really hadn't a clue. A throwback to his undercover days. "I knew you'd go out tonight after Andy, so I'm going with you. Even bought boots at Horn to Hoof. The saleslady said the Dawsons are getting to be one of their best customers."

Maggie slid between the rungs of the fence, picked the saddle from him and heaved it onto Butterfly, then said, "Okay, where is it?"

"Where's what?"

"I slept this afternoon, but I'll bet our firstborn you didn't. You went back into town, didn't you. You went to the sheriff's office to see Roy."

He didn't even have time to get his innocent look in place before she started patting him down, first one shirt pocket, then the other. He didn't mind, of course. Hell, he loved it, until her hands on his chest started turning him on more than he'd been turned on in a long time. Not that he hadn't been with women; he just hadn't been with *this* woman. "Wh-what are you after?"

"A silver star." She reached into his back pocket, her hands on his butt, turning him on even more. When she went for his front jeans pocket he figured he had to come clean or be embarrassed when she found something she wasn't looking for at all. How would he explain *that?*

"Here," he said, yanking the star from his front jeans pocket. "I assume that's what you want."

Maggie kicked at the dirt. "I knew when I landed on the floor of the café you were going to do the sheriff thing no matter what I said. You can't help yourself. You're a copaholic." She held out the star. "Give it back."

He shook his head. "Roy can't keep up and I can help. I don't want you to worry. Nothing's going to happen, and Roy can ride out with you to make sure it doesn't."

Her brows furrowed. "So what are you doing here with a saddle in your hand if Roy's the one who's riding out with me?"

"Well, tonight there's a glitch. Roy's kids are in a play at school. He's in town watching the—"

"And you're going with me?" She pursed her lips. "No need for that. My hands are with me. I'll be fine. And considering your track record of attracting unsavory sorts, I'm probably safer *without* you than with you."

He would not pout. "Hey, I don't always attract trouble."

"I never ended up on the floor of the Purple Sage until you showed up. Then there's the bank and Vegas to consider. And that's just what I know about." She slipped the star back into his pocket and patted it. "You have the night off, Sheriff Jack Dawson."

JACK PACED the porch…his newest and most pathetic habit since he'd arrived in Whistlers Bend. At least Ben was home, having made curfew by the skin of his teeth. And the parents had decided to spend the night in Stillwater, so they were okay. But where the hell was Maggie?

How many times had he asked *that* question in the past twenty-four hours? A lot more than he'd thought he would have; that was for damn sure. He'd always pictured her in her big log house or in the barns or petting a cow or some other ranch thing that was peaceful and calm. Not riding the range like Clint Eastwood. It was never this way in Chicago. He'd never paced there. *Hell, she had…over him.*

How'd she survive worrying about him like this day after day, year after year? He hadn't realized till this very moment what she'd been going through. No wonder she'd left him. He wondered why she hadn't left sooner.

He couldn't stomach Maggie missing for another second. Even if she was with her hands, something could happen to her. He'd saddle up Butterfly if it took all night, and then he'd ride out and find Maggie if he had to yell her name till he was hoarse and—

But he wouldn't have to do that, because she suddenly rounded the corner of the barn, leading her horse, both of them limping.

His heart dropped to his toes, and he broke out in a full sweat. Maggie hurt twice in one day? Maybe he *was* a trouble magnet. He jumped from the porch to the ground and ran toward her, his legs not moving as fast as he wanted, his lungs on fire.

He pulled up in front of her by the barn door, out of breath more from fear than running. He noticed scratches on her face, her ripped jacket and blood on her hands. He turned them over and over again, his heart like a rock in his chest.

"What the hell happened? Where were the cowboys who help you? Who did this to you, Maggie? I'll string them up. Have a necktie party. Isn't that what sheriffs do to the bad guys in the West?"

"Not for about a hundred years now, and you don't have to string up anybody. One of the fences got cut. I tried to help mend it instead of letting the hands do it, as I should have. But I'm a forty-year-old control freak and have to be knee-deep into everything myself. The barbed wire snapped. I was in the way and—"

"A fence? This happened because of a damn fence?"

"A damn cut fence, but we scared off the guys who did it before they got any of the cows or calves, so that's the good part—"

"You scared them? Who's 'them'? *Hell, Maggie.* I...you... Ah, dammit all, woman, you drive me crazy." He snatched her into his arms and kissed her hard.

Chapter Four

No man on the face of the earth kissed like Jack Dawson.
Not that Maggie had kissed all that many guys in her life,
but how could any other man improve on perfection? The
intimate feel of Jack's mouth on hers, his unique male
scent, made her wild with wanting him. His firm body
and commanding embrace, which said he knew just how
to hold a woman as if he possessed her body and soul,
the hint of danger in his all-around rugged appearance,
overwhelmed her...just as they always had.

How could Jack's intense kisses *still* do this? Being
overwhelmed by him should be an outgrown condition
like...like losing teeth or acne.

Then his arms tightened, arousing her to breathless-
ness. This was...sex. Pure, hormones-on-a-rampage,
mutual-attraction hot sex between two adults.

Her nipples hardened against his muscled chest—
she'd forgotten they could do that. Her insides ached
for wanting him closer still to satisfy a need she hadn't
known was there till right now. She'd had two semi-
serious relationships since her divorce, but neither of

those guys had affected her like this. She had the uncontrollable urge to tackle Jack to the ground right here, tear off his shirt and pants and other pieces of apparel that kept her from running her hands over every wonderful steely-hard male inch of him and... and...

What the heck was wrong with her? She'd never wanted to tear men's clothes off before, except for Jack's, and that was a long, long, long time ago. She pulled her head back and gulped in a lungful of air, suddenly dizzy. "This isn't a good idea, Jack."

"We've had worse." His voice was low and rough as his gaze met hers and a sly grin tipped his lips. "Or not. I don't care."

Crickets chirped and the bushes stirred. His eyes darted from one side to the other and she watched him instinctively reach for his gun. "What was that?"

"Opossum, raccoon, fox...fleeting good sense."

His arms dropped away from her, exposing her to the night chill—pitiful replacement for his hot body on hers. He raked back his hair. "You scare the hell out of me, Maggie." His eyes hardened a fraction. "You shouldn't have gone off alone."

Arguing. Okay, she could handle arguing with Jack. The kissing part knocked her for a loop. *No more kissing.* She could not get tangled up with him, only to separate again when he left. Tearing her heart out once like that was enough...way more than enough.

"Look, I got caught in a fence, and unless you're

good at repairing barbed wire you wouldn't have been any help to me or anyone else."

"What would have happened if you'd come on those guys when they were cutting the fence, huh? If they didn't hightail it out of there when you and the hands arrived? What were you going to do then? Talk to them? That *is* your great strategy, right?" He waved toward the range. "This isn't the UN, dammit."

"If it's somebody I know, I talk. But if I don't recognize the person I don't charge in like the cavalry. I'm not crazy, Jack. I just don't want to make trouble if I can help it."

She swiped her hair from her face. "We have a different take on things in Whistlers Bend. The Saint Valentine's Day Massacre means going to Candies and Cream on February fourteenth and gorging on chocolates, not mowing people down in the middle of the street."

"Mowing is history, except for grass. Chicago's not like that now."

She gave him a wide-eyed, disbelieving look.

"Okay, *usually* it's not like that. But Whistlers Bend isn't utopia, either. I'll take care of the horse. Go get cleaned up."

"JD's thrown a shoe. That's why I was walking instead of riding. I'll have to get the smithy over."

"JD?" Jack's eyes suddenly lit with a flash of humor. "Miss me that much?"

She pursed her lips. "What an ego. JD is for Just Dandy," she lied. She hoped she wasn't blushing, giv-

ing herself away that *JD* indeed stood for Jack Dawson—though she told everyone it meant *Just Dandy.*
"You *do* know how to unsaddle a horse?"

"Hey, saddle and unsaddle…I got that part down,
sort of. It's what happens in between that's busting my
chops." His eyes turned hard, that no-messing-around-
now cop look firmly back in place. "Don't do this again,
Maggie."

"I will if I have to, Jack."

She walked to the house, trying not to limp as she
stepped up onto the porch. She opened the door and took
the stairs to her bedroom, massaging her knee as she
went. How could she get tangled up in a fence? She'd
been around fences all her life…except her Chicago
life. She considered the ranch, her ranch. Why had she
ever thought she could live in Chicago when she'd had
all this here?

Jack Dawson, that was why. She'd loved him enough
to live on the moon if she could be with him…until
she'd realized what being a cop's wife entailed. Simply,
the constant worry had eaten her alive.

She peeled off clothes, ran the shower hot and
climbed in. A moan slid up her throat as the water eased
her aches. Hot showers, one of life's greatest inven-
tions, the next best thing to sex.

Her eyes flew open. *Sex! No sex!* She was not going
there. Not after the barn encounter.

She concentrated on her cuts and scrapes, which
stung as she washed them clean. 'Course, they were
nothing like the ones Jack used to bring home. Patch-

ing him up had gotten to be a regular occurrence. Then he'd head for the shower, her at his side, soon surrounded by billowing steam and mounds of slippery suds and slippery hands searching for a place to…slip.

He'd wash her hair; she'd return the favor and do his, bubbles sliding down his wonderful, powerful body. His hands gliding over her face, her throat, her breasts, her navel, sliding to her thighs, then between them as she spread her legs and…

She flipped the shower to cold and gasped. *Eight more days of this!* She should have sent Jack pictures of Ben's graduation, not invited him here! Never in a million years had she expected to get so involved with Jack Dawson again, to the point where she couldn't even take a shower without thinking about him, every delicious inch of him. No, not delicious. She was over Jack Dawson. *Over, over, over!*

She dried off, then wrapped her hair in a towel and pulled on her robe. Sucked in a breath, rubbed a clear spot on the steamed mirror with the sleeve of her robe and gave herself one more pep talk on being over Jack. Then she squared her shoulders, opened the door to the bathroom, feeling more in control—and collided with him, their bodies so close a paper clip couldn't squeeze between.

All capacity to think rationally vanished. She should have stayed in the cold shower.

"I was just coming to get you."

"Get me?" she squeaked. She swallowed, a flash of desire sending her heart racing.

He held up a yellow-and-blue tube and smiled. "Antibacterial cream."

Relief, or maybe frustration, made her weak. Jack Dawson was driving her insane. She didn't know what to expect from him or herself.

"You still keep the first-aid kit in the kitchen, same place as when we were married. Thought I'd pay you back for all the times you patched me back together."

She peered at him. "Aren't we mad at each other? Didn't we just have a fight outside over me doing my thing and you not liking it?" Of course, they'd also had one dynamite kiss.

"We had a disagreement and you need to put something on those cuts."

He straightened the lapel on her terry-cloth robe, his lingering fingers looking very male against the pink material. "Can't believe you still have this old thing. What Christmas did I give it to you?"

She licked her lips, which felt dry as a creek bed in July. "Birthday."

"Yeah, birthday. The last one we were together." Sadness and regret flashed across his face.

She wanted to touch him, tell him it was okay. They'd split up because they had to. They both understood that. Their divorce wasn't bitter, angry. Just necessary, before they destroyed each other. But with eight days stretching before them, saying all that would be like upsetting a canoe with no shore in sight. "I...I think I know how they got Andy."

That must be the best mood-breaking line of all times!

Jack's face relaxed. "Andy? Yeah, that's good. That's great, in fact. That you figured out how they got him, I mean."

She took a step back just as he did, as if they both realized the hornet's nest was best left alone. "Since you don't just throw a rope over a buffalo and say come-along-little dogie. They must have used Peeps."

He unscrewed the top from the cream and put it on the nightstand. "Peeps as in some sort of oat concoction?" He squeezed a dollop onto his fingers.

Oh, no. Jack putting the cream on her skin would not work. Stroking was *not* a good idea, especially when it followed a hot kiss, erotic shower images and body-to-body contact.

Jack must have had the same thought, because all of a sudden he looked as though he didn't know what to do with the ointment. She smiled, snatched the tube and wiped the cream from his fingers onto her own. "I can do this. I can feel where the scrapes are."

Her brain didn't compute scrapes at the moment, so she slapped the cream on her face, hoping it landed somewhere it was needed. "Peeps are marshmallow cutouts dunked in colored sugar."

"Marshmallows with sugar?" He folded his arms across his chest. His eyes now held a twinkle instead of the fire there minutes earlier.

Good. Fire and Jack were an unsettling, irresistible mix. "I'm not kidding."

She slid up the sleeve of her robe and concentrated on applying the cream. "BJ's addicted to the things, but don't say a word to anyone, because it's bad for a doctor's image. A junk-food-eating doctor loses respect, especially when she's peddling fruits and veggies. Anyway, one day she fed Andy a handful of Peeps and he nearly brought the fence down to get the rest."

"Buffalo eat marshmallows?"

"Buffalo eat anything they want. Ever try to tell a buffalo no? Peeps are how *I* get Andy to go where I want him to. He'd follow a bag of those things to California."

She put the cream on her other arm. "So, by using brilliant deductive reasoning, I'm sure whoever snagged Andy used Peeps. Ta-da!"

"You missed a spot." Before she could stop him, he swiped cream from the tube and touched a scrape on her nose. His eyes on her face; her eyes on him; the cream cooling her skin, which seemed heated from the inside out. She'd hoped the great Peeps conversation would bore Jack to death, make him yawn and leave the room in a near-coma state.

He wasn't leaving and was nowhere near a coma.

His touch was caring…tender. Just as she remembered. Why did she have to remember? Why couldn't she forget? She shivered.

"Cold?"

Not exactly.

"You realize what this means, don't you?"

That you can turn me on with one look, one stroke of your finger, one silly comment? "Andy's going to get cavities?"

He grinned as he dabbed cream on a spot on her

forehead. "Whoever borrowed Andy knew about the candy, which means the job was local, someone who's a friend or neighbor or they wouldn't have known where to find Andy in the first place. You keep him fenced off from the rest of the herd, right?"

"The cows and new calves are on the middle range and we have Andy in a pasture. Unless someone knew where to look, it would take time to find any of the herd. This is called the wide-open spaces for a reason."

He rubbed cream into her hands, the warmth radiating all the way up her arms and beyond. "It also has to be someone who doesn't want you to succeed. Got any ideas what that might be?"

"I like my cavity answer a whole lot more, because I hate to believe someone would be after me this way. I can't imagine why. My herd only affects my business. Some other ranchers may not like what I'm doing, but it's not as if I'm forcing my ideas on them. The beef industry of old will continue to flourish. Beefalo is a niche that should work for Sky Notch."

He took the tube and recapped it. "Until we figure out what's going on, you'll have to be more careful. Somebody's got it in for you, Maggie. It's personal, whether to force you into bankruptcy or discourage you from experimenting with other breeds. You're in danger more than you're aware."

She looked at Jack. *Danger? Mostly because you're here.* The man had *danger* written all over him and her being naked under a threadbare robe didn't offer much in the way of safety, considering she wanted nothing more than to drop the blasted robe and attack him.

He touched her cheek. "There. I think you'll live."

Not likely, since death from uncontrolled desire was imminent. But since she couldn't say that, she went with, "Good night, Jack, and thanks."

JACK WALKED from Maggie's room toward his. Touching her was torture, leaving him as horny as a Chicago traffic jam. How could applying antibacterial cream be so seductive? His erection pressed against his zipper, making him wince with every step. Maybe he shouldn't have come to Whistlers Bend in the first place.

But not attending Ben's graduation would make him more of an absentee father, and not being around his son made Jack feel guilty enough.

No, the problem wasn't that he'd come. The problem was he'd kissed Maggie, lathered her with cream and stirred feelings he didn't need stirred. Feelings he'd worked so damn hard to forget or at least bury.

For the next eight days the only thing between him and Maggie was Ben. Not how wonderful she felt in his arms, or that she still wore the robe he'd given her, or how beautiful she was in the moonlight, or how much he liked being with her or how attracted he felt to her even after all these years of being apart.

Incredible as it seemed, forty-something Maggie appealed to him even more than the twenty-something Maggie. She had a goal and went after it all by herself. Her ability to get the job done, being successful in her own right and respected and resourceful as hell, appealed to him in a big way. He appreciated that she took pride in her work and that others valued her opinion and tenacity. But as long as he stayed in Whistlers Bend, he'd keep his mind on Ben and graduation, and not on his attraction to Maggie.

Of course he'd stick with his plan to keep her safe— he had to do that. But he'd stay emotionally uninvolved. He'd be a Chicago cop in Montana. Nothing more, nothing less. Just do his job and get the hell out of Dodge, or in this case Whistlers Bend, when the time came for him to leave. He fell asleep as he decided that was his best plan.

And as the first rays of sunlight peeked over the mountains, waking Jack from a sound sleep, he felt more sure than ever his plan to stay aloof from Maggie but offer protection would work fine. He'd headed up tough assignments and always maintained a professional distance. He'd think of this as one more assignment and then go back to Chicago.

He shrugged into jeans, threw on a T-shirt and barefooted it down the steps toward the massive kitchen. Hell, his whole apartment could probably fit in that kitchen. Then again, if the wonderful aromas emanating from the room were any indication, Maggie spent more time in this kitchen than he ever did in his apartment.

He followed the scent of strong coffee and freshbaked things and entered a kitchen festooned with pies, cakes, cupcakes and doughnuts. Maggie hauled a sheet of cookies from the oven, then slid in another.

Uh-oh. Not a good sign. He went still and asked, "What's wrong?"

She blew a limp strand of hair from her forehead and snatched up a spatula. "I'm fine."

"Like hell. When something goes haywire, you bake. You bake a *lot*. Guys at the precinct mourned our divorce for months. No more cakes, pies, cookies." He studied her. "Are the scratches causing you problems? Is that why you're baking? Are the parents okay? *What?*"

She flipped cookies to a rack like the expert she was. "Dad called and they're doing breakfast at the Purple Sage. Our son's what's causing me problems, and as soon as I get my hands on him I intend to cause him so many problems he won't know which end's up."

Jack felt his heart freeze, his chest contract into a painful knot, as parenthood—the real side of parenthood—crashed down around him. "What happened to Ben? Is he all right?" Jack could barely get the words out. A totally stupid reaction. If anything was critically wrong, Maggie would be with Ben, not here, elbow-deep in flour, butter and sugar. Panic seized him all the same.

"He didn't come home last night."

Jack sat on the bar stool at the counter, feeling sort of faint. He couldn't talk. Couldn't think.

She pointed the spatula at the phone. "I've called every sheriff's department and hospital within a fifty-mile radius. He's not there and no one's seen him. But that doesn't mean he's not in a ditch or—" She put down the cookie sheet. Her gaze met Jack's, and the worry in her eyes nearly did him in. She swallowed. "He has a cell phone, dammit. Why didn't he call me?"

She went as white as the icing on the oatmeal cookies. Jack stood and put his arm around her shoulders, not feeling stable himself.

"I should never have divorced you."

Of all the things she might say, *that* one he hadn't counted on. Her head snapped up and she faced him, her mouth pinched.

"If we lived in Chicago this wouldn't have happened. You would have been around. Ben would have had the father he loves and deserves. I've been too easy on him, spending too much time with the herd, then Dad and raising Andy and—"

He cuddled her closer. "Don't do this to yourself, Maggie." He kissed her forehead. "I didn't give you much reason to stay in Chicago."

"I wimped out. I've thought about not staying so many times and wondered if... But instead I ran home. I should never have let Ben out last night."

"He's eighteen. You can't lock him in his room, no matter how tempting the idea is. In three months he's off to college."

"Oh, God. College." She sat on a bar stool. "I'll never survive college." The phone rang and she snagged the receiver with the lightning speed that would do a Chicago Cubs shortstop proud. It was Ben. He was all right. From the gist of the conversation, Jack could

piece together that Ben had fallen asleep on his girl-friend's couch and forgotten to call.

Anger pooled in Jack's gut as he watched color return to Maggie's face. Anger at himself for not helping with Ben more and anger at Ben for being so inconsiderate of his mother.

She hung up, stared at Jack. "He's at school now, which is a good thing. I can calm down and talk rationally when he gets home this afternoon. That's eight hours away. I need eight hours to get myself together."

She smiled. "I'll fix you French toast. You still like French toast, don't you? I have real maple syrup."

He'd like nothing better than French toast and maple syrup. "I have an errand to run."

She wagged her finger, as if knowing his thoughts. "Jack. Don't do this. I recognize that look. Don't bother Ben at school. I'll handle it when he gets home. You don't have to show up and be the bad guy. That's not fair to you. You haven't been in Whistlers Bend in ten years and you don't have to be the heavy."

He kissed her hair, loving the way it smelled of vanilla and all things homey. "I think it's time for one of those little father-son chats."

She sighed. "Jack? I can—"

He cupped her chin in his hand and gazed into her wonderful blue eyes, still blurred with worry. A long time ago it had been because of him, now it was because of Ben. He hated seeing her this way. That was why he'd let her go in the first place and hadn't pleaded with her to stay. He couldn't stand the look of terror that seemed

to go all the way to her soul. "I'm sure you can do anything, Maggie. But it's my turn. It was my turn years ago
and I just didn't take it."

He kissed her on the cheek. Liked it so much he
kissed her on the lips, loving the feel of her full, moist
mouth against his. 'Course, that sent his great plan to
be nothing but a cop straight to hell, but he'd fish it out
later. He grabbed a handful of oatmeal-with-raisin cookies, then gave her a reassuring grin and a two-fingered
salute as he headed for shoes and a shirt.

Fifteen minutes later Jack parked the Suburban in front
of Whistlers Bend High School. He dusted cookie crumbs
from his shirt, ruffled his hair and smiled at his good for-
tune at not having shaved yet. Never underestimate the
power of intimidation, and he was the master of that.

No one stopped him as he entered the building. Either security sucked or they all knew him already and
weren't about to deal with a thoroughly pissed-off Jack
Dawson. How smart on their part.

He made his way to the office and approached the
secretary. Small, fifty-something, tidy, wise with a no-
nonsense air about her. The perfect high school secretary. The office went still as he said, "I'm Benjamin
Dawson's father. I'd like to see him. Just for a few
minutes, if it's not too much trouble. He forgot something."

A twinkle lit the secretary's pale blue eyes. "Maggie
called. More fathers should see their kids when they 'forget something.' I'll get Benjamin for you, Detective Dawson. Would you like to speak to him in one of our offices?"

As in most schools, the secretary was the one who kept the place going. Overworked, underpaid, destined for sainthood. "This won't be long."

The woman smiled, a chuckle in her voice as she said, "No, I don't think it will."

He stood by the wall to wait as the office returned to the hustle and bustle of education. And then Ben was there.

"Dad." His son didn't seem all that surprised to see Jack was there. News, all news, traveled fast in Whistlers Bend, especially big, ugly, unshaven news.

"Son. Let's take a little walk around the school."

Ben's eyes bulged. Had he stopped breathing? *Good.* Dirty jeans, shirt no better, mussed hair, needed a shave, hands in his pockets. Jack realized his own hands were in his pockets and his shoulders hunched forward…just like Ben's. Father and son and identical as those cutout cookies Maggie made. Ben was Jack twenty-three years ago. He considered his life then. *Oh, hell.* This was payback for all the grief he'd caused his own father.

Jack dropped a strong arm around his son and guided him out of the office and though the double glass doors of the school building.

"Look, Dad," Ben started to say when they got to the sidewalk. "I was wrong. I should have called Mom. But I helped a girl move and it got late and I fell asleep." He reddened. "On her couch…alone."

Ben shifted his weight to his other foot…about the same time Jack did. Uncanny as hell.

"Did Mom bake?"

Jack nodded.

Ben sighed. "Cripes. I'd hoped she wouldn't bake."

Jack fought to keep his eyes from widening with surprise. "You know about that?"

Ben shrugged. "She bakes all the time. The Betty Crocker of Whistlers Bend. Makes up her own recipes. She should franchise." Ben swallowed. "I'll apologize to her as soon as I get home. It won't happen again, I swear. I wouldn't hurt Mom like that. I screwed up."

"Who's this girl?"

Ben raked a hand through his hair, making it more of a mess. Jack guessed it mirrored his at the moment. "You'll have to trust me on this one, Dad. I got this covered…except for not calling. That was dumb. Really dumb. I'm sorry. I'll do better."

"Are you sleeping with her?"

Ben's jaw dropped, his eyes bulged. "No. Hell, no!"

"Are you bullshitting me? Because if you're out there having unprotected sex and—"

"I would never do that, and that's not what this is all about. I'll tell you what's going on when I can. I just can't right now. This girl's a friend. That's all, a friend. And she trusts me and I'm asking you to do the same."

"You got a week, then I want answers." He peered at his son. "And if you're the cause of your mother baking any more cookies, pies, cakes or whatever before I go, she'll be serving them at your funeral. Got it?"

Ben nodded. "Got it."

Jack watched his son walk back toward the school. Before the boy opened the door he turned, the expression in his brown eyes bright, sincere, determined. "You've got cookie crumbs on your sleeve, Dad." He flashed a lopsided grin and gave a two-fingered salute, then went inside.

Holy crap! DNA ran strong and deep. Incredible stuff. How could he have missed his son growing up? How could he not have followed Maggie to Whistlers Bend? But what the hell would he have done here had he come? He heaved a mental sigh. Too late to worry about any of those things now.

Jack drove back to the ranch and parked beside the barn. Henry moseyed down the wide front steps of the porch and walked his way, cupcake in one hand, coffee in the other. "How'd it go? Maggie told me what happened but didn't want to worry your folks. Did you give Ben one of those *I brought you into this world I can take you out* speeches?"

Jack chuckled. "Yeah, the take-out speech is pretty much how it went." He nodded at the cupcake. "Didn't think you were allowed to have those things."

"I'm not." He took a bite and smiled, sheer delight in his eyes. Then he said around a mouthful of crumbs, "But how can I resist such a spread of goodies. Edward and Gert are trying to find containers for everything inside. We'll drop some off with some of the folks in town. Maggie hasn't baked like this in two years, since she got back from seeing you in the hospital and—"

Henry stopped midchew. His smile slipped a notch. "Ah, hell."

For the second time this morning, Jack felt as if he'd

been whacked in the gut with a small car. "Maggie was in Chicago? *Two years ago?*"

"Ah, double hell."

"The hospital?"

"Yeah, and she's going to skin me alive for letting the cat out of the bag. It's those cupcakes. Lose my head when I eat triple-chocolate cupcakes. Some people get a yappy mouth when they drink too much. For me it's chocolate. Think I'd know better after all these years. I need to join Chocoholics Anonymous and—"

"Henry, when was Maggie in Chicago?"

"You're not letting up on this, are you?"

Jack answered with a tough look.

"Damn. It was that time you got caught in the cross-fire and wound up taking a bullet in the chest." Henry sipped the coffee and smacked his lips. "Or was that the time before, when you got shot in—"

"She came more than once?"

Henry rolled his shoulders. "Well now. How many times have you been in the hospital? Edward calls when you wind up there. We all keep in touch. I know Maggie's racked up a ton of frequent flyer miles. Next visit she can go first class."

He peered at Jack and shook his head. "Not that we want there to be a next time—least, not under those circumstances."

Maggie had come to see him? When he'd dreamed she'd been there beside him in the hospital, touching him, it hadn't been dreams at all? "Why was she there? Why didn't someone tell me? Why didn't you?"

"Hell, I just did…even if I didn't mean to. You need to ask her the rest of those questions. Not sure why the folks in Chicago kept her visits confidential. But I bet brownies were involved."

"Where is she?" Exasperation tightened his chest.

Henry hitched his chin toward the barn. "Rode out while you were gone. Said to tell you not to worry. Nothing's going to happen in broad daylight and she'll be back here in a few hours. And you were welcome to hang Ben's hide over the fireplace if you had a mind to."

"She rode out alone *again?*" His eyes widened to his hairline.

"When the ranch hands returned from fixing the barbed-wire fence they said they'd found tire tracks in the dirt. She wanted to follow them before the rain hit. Maybe Andy's at the other end."

Jack swiped his hand over his face. "Does that woman *ever* stay in one place?"

Henry laughed. "Not for very long, I can vouch for that. Wears me out just watching her."

Jack wasn't sure what drove him crazier—wanting to know about Maggie's visits to Chicago, or her not taking someone along again. Didn't they just have the talk about the business with Andy being a local job? Someone she knew and how that was dangerous? "I'm going out to get her."

He gazed at the grass, the rolling hills, the sky and far-off mountains. "Uh, where…where do I go? Is there a map or something?"

"Map?" Henry licked chocolate icing from his fingers. "See that cut in the mountains up there?" He pointed at the western horizon, to a gash in the rocks. "Head for that—you should run right into the fence line. My guess is Maggie won't be far away. She doesn't have that much of a head start, and you should be able to spot her. The area's flat there. Just take a look around and holler. No need getting in a lather. If she finds something suspicious she'll get Roy."

"Maybe. Maybe not. Depends on what kind of obstinate mood she happens to be in."

Henry shrugged. "Maggie tends to do what she damn well pleases these days."

"No kidding!"

"Women turn forty and suddenly have a mind all their own. They're smart, self-assured and don't give a tinker's damn what anyone else thinks. They're not out to impress anyone but themselves, and they do it."

He winked at Jack. "You should have come to Whistlers Bend five years ago, boy. Maggie wasn't so headstrong then."

"Yeah, well I'm here now and I'll have to deal with it." He pulled himself up straight. "I'm a Chicago cop. I can handle this, I'm sure."

Henry laughed. "You just keep telling yourself that."

He followed Jack into the barn and saddled up Butterfly a lot easier with the horse in the stall and after watching Maggie and Henry. Jack mounted, and Henry put the reins in his hands. "Slide these through your fingers and hold on to them like you mean business. Get an attitude about you. Imagine that Butterfly just ran three traffic lights on Michigan Avenue and you're hell-bent on stopping his ass before he does it again."

"I can relate to that."

"That's what I figured." Henry slid his cowboy hat from his head and gave it to Jack. "Keeps the sun out of your eyes."

Jack put it on and pushed it this way and that. "Doesn't feel right."

"A Stetson is something you have to grow into, kind of like Montana. You'll get used to both before you know it. Give 'em time."

"Save me a cupcake. One with sprinkles on top." He nudged Butterfly, held on and, wonder of wonders, the horse took off in a steady trot.

Jack pulled the Stetson down tighter so it wouldn't bounce off. Henry yelled, "Balance on the balls of your feet, boy, and grip with your legs. Get a rhythm, or you won't sit for a week."

Jack bounced. When Butterfly went up, Jack's butt came down, jarring his whole body to the fillings of his teeth. His head hurt, his neck snapped, his butt would never recover. Impotence seemed a real possibility.

Wide-open spaces took on a whole new meaning. Trees, rocks, bright blue skies overhead, puffs of clouds, warm sun, grass everywhere. 'Course they were all going up and down. His head felt as though it belonged on a bobble doll; still, for the next hour he aimed for the cut in the mountain as best he could.

He could see which mountain and which cut because the sunlight reflected off one side, and then suddenly clouds crawled over the mountaintops, blocking the sun and making all the mountains look sort of gray and brown and way too much alike.

Jack reined in Butterfly and looked around now that things had quit moving. Grass, grass, grass. Clouds, clouds, clouds. Mountains, mountains, mountains. Everything looked exactly alike. A sign that said This Way would be good here. *Damn good.* So would a chiropractor.

Jack was completely lost and totally bewildered. He'd never felt lost or bewildered in Chicago. Thunder rumbled in the distance. Was it calling him dumb-ass for venturing out into the middle of flipping nowhere?

Well, that was too damn bad. Dumb-ass or not, he needed to find Maggie. At least, that was the plan until a crack of lightning split the gray sky like a shot from a gun. Another flash zigzagged, hitting a pine tree in the distance, making it spark like fireworks on the Fourth of July. Butterfly reared and Jack found himself staring at the sky.

"Holy hell!" He held on for all he was worth, trying to stay in the saddle, then the horse took off in a dead run for God knows where.

Chapter Five

Maggie hunkered down behind the old dilapidated, weather-scarred train depot at Silver Gulch and pushed her Stetson to the back of her head as she studied the fresh tire tracks in the dirt. Yet as she stared at the ground, she wasn't really seeing anything, because visions of Jack Dawson invaded her brain.

No matter how hard she tried to concentrate on other things, it didn't happen. *Blast that kiss.* It had brought back memories of how things used to be between them. Their marriage hadn't been *all* worry and frustration. When Jack had come home to her and Ben, things had seemed wonderful. Going out for pizza, to Navy Pier, the Art Institute and the Shedd were magic times filled with so much fun and love. Definitely love.

Sometimes when he slept and she couldn't, she'd sketch him, mesmerized by the peaceful expression on his face. She'd kept those pictures, framed her favorite and put it in the hallway.

Why couldn't he have retired from the police force

at twenty-eight? But then what would he have done? Jack Dawson equaled cop, period!

Focus, Maggie, focus. On the tracks, *not Jack.* She poked at the dust. Yep, the treads were the same as the ones she'd followed from the cut in the fence. Did Butch have a truck with this tread? Dan Pruitt might know, since he lived close. Too bad she didn't have one of those plaster kits she'd seen on police shows on TV, where they take impressions of tire tracks. Maybe she could draw them…*if* she had pencil and paper.

She stood and followed the tracks a little farther, leading Cisco around the side of the depot. The tracks suddenly mixed with other tire tracks, wider ones. A bigger truck? Butch didn't have a truck this big. The fat tracks veered off in one direction, the narrow tracks in another. As if the two vehicles had parked, then gone off but not together. Or maybe there was no connection at all and they'd arrived and left at different times. At this rate she'd never find Andy!

A fat raindrop plopped in the middle of the path, making a dark brown dot. A gust rustled the scraggly bushes and overgrown weeds. She studied the sky as it faded from cornflower-blue to dust-bunny–gray. Storms weren't expected till evening. It wasn't even noon. That weatherperson needed to stick his or her head out the window once in a while. More drops fell, turning dirt to mud and obliterating the treads right before her eyes.

This never happened on *CSI.* They got tire prints and caught the bad guy in one hour. One stinking hour. Andy was MIA four days now.

What kind of mean-spirited person would steal her Andy? She had raised him, fed him from a bottle so he'd get to know her and she could handle him better when he grew up. Someone had stolen her baby and she intended to get the no-good bastard if it took forever.

Lightning zigzagged over the Beartooth Mountains. Thunder rumbled, shaking the earth with a deep rattle that vibrated right up the valley. Cisco whinnied as he shook his mane and pawed the dirt. He gave Maggie a *how dare you have me out in this rotten weather* look.

"You're right. Let's get out of here."

She led him around front of the depot and onto the porch, his hooves making hollow sounds on the rotting wood floorboards. She pushed open the door suspended on one rusted hinge and coaxed Cisco inside. "This won't last too long. Storms that are fast in are fast out. You know that."

She settled him into a corner where he couldn't see the storm since horses and lightning were a bad mix. Then she perched herself in the doorway to watch nature's show. Cisco might not like Montana storms blowing across the range, but she considered them the greatest show on earth, providing you had shelter and weren't out in the open like some human lightning rod.

Clouds piled in great masses till she couldn't see where earth ended and sky began. A strong gust blew and she took off her hat, letting her hair stream back and the wind cool her heated skin. Dead weeds and brush somersaulted across the ground, dust spiraled and danced over the open ground. And was that a rider approaching from the west? He was heading straight for the depot and riding like a bat out of hell. Though it wasn't exactly *riding* so much as holding on for dear life.

She stood, gazing into the gloom as the rider jerked side to side. Some city slicker, no doubt. But who... "Butterfly?" Her eyes widened. "Jack? Holy heck it *is* Jack."

At least Butterfly knew where to go for shelter. He galloped flat out till he got to the depot, did a straight-legged halt right in front of the place, Jack nearly careering over the horse's head in the whiplash stop.

Butterfly then gingerly stepped up onto the porch to get out of the rain, causing Jack to lose his hat on the overhang.

Shoulders bent, he stared at the floorboards, not moving. "This horse hates me."

She retrieved the hat, shook the water from it, then looked up at him. He still wasn't moving. "What in the world are you doing out here?"

"Getting damn wet."

His focus shifted and he glared at her, his eyes sort of rolling around in his head. "Before that I was searching for you, till this poor excuse for an animal decided rain was not his bag and ran off like the devil wanted us for dinner. Good thing I already have a son, because after this ride, I'm sure my fathering days are over."

For a second she remembered those days, when they'd decided to have a family and the fun they'd had making that decision a reality. "Why don't you get down."

"Legs won't work. Butt's numb. Head on a pogo stick. Give me a minute."

She took the reins and held Butterfly in place. "Just swing your leg over and slide on your stomach."

He shot her a sideways glance. "Hummer. Think Hummer. Big, big car. Goes where you want it to go. Complete with key and steering wheel." He lowered himself onto the porch. His legs wobbled as he steadied against the side of the depot.

"You okay?"

"Damn terrific."

She kissed his cheek for comfort, but the feel of her lips on his wet, rough flesh sidestepped comfort and went straight to warm, wild and sexy. She stepped back and swallowed a gasp. How could an innocent kiss do that? Then she considered the kisser and the kissee and had her answer. The two of them had left innocence behind a long time ago.

She led Butterfly into the depot beside Cisco. "You guys stay calm. This will be over soon." She thought of Jack and heat sizzled through her. "I hope."

She pulled a towel, blanket and water from her saddlebags, then glanced to the doorway. Jack leaned against the beam that supported the remaining part of the porch. Broad shouldered, thick torsoed, tough. She swallowed. Not always tough. Sometimes gentle, caring, intimate. Darn, did she have to consider intimate?

More lightning lit the sky as she went back outside. A torrent of rain hammered the tin roof like rocks dropped from a tall place. *Think ordinary, mundane conversation,* she ordered herself. She forced a smile and turned to him. "You just made it in time. The open prairie is no place to be in a storm." She handed him the towel and a blanket.

His eyes widened. "Where'd these come from?"

"Saddlebags. You never know what's going to happen out here. Be prepared and all that. Would you like some water?"

"I've had my quota for the day." He dropped the blanket in a dry spot. "You wouldn't happen to have a beer in those saddlebags, would you?"

She leaned against a wall and watched him dry off, just as she had so many times before. Though now he had clothes on. She pictured him the other way, the without-clothes way. She used to watch just to appreciate his...maleness. And did he have terrific maleness! Firm thighs, strong wide back, great butt, really great equipment on the opposite side.

"Maggie?"

Her eyes met his. *Drat!*

"Are you okay?"

Heck no! Needing to get her mind off Jack's fabulous anatomy, she stared at the rain streaming off the metal roof. "Bet you haven't seen a storm like this. Even the ones that blow in off the lake in Chicago don't measure up to a Montana storm, least as far as I can remember."

"You can't remember two years ago?"

She cut her eyes back to him. A chill snaked up her back. *Uh-oh.* She stopped herself from nibbling her bottom lip in obvious guilt. "Two years? What's with two years?"

A touch of fire and a hint of danger flashed across his controlled cop face—something that didn't happen very often. "Yeah, when you came to see me in the hospital."

He braced his arms against the depot, one on either side of her, caging her. Her heart pounded. Best to play it cool. Maybe he was just fishing. Cops did that. Fishing experts. *Act innocent.* "Why would I go to Chicago?"

"You tell me."

Blast! How'd he know about Chicago? "Dad!" She rolled her eyes and huffed, needing to say something, *anything,* with Jack so close, the heat of his body radiating into hers, exciting hers, turning her on. *Holy moly!* "He's been eating triple-chocolate cupcakes again, hasn't he? He forgets himself when he eats chocolate. You never know what he's going to say. I baked him low-fat no-cholesterol cupcakes of his very own, but does he eat them? Heck no, he goes for—"

Jack claimed her mouth in a demanding, no-nonsense kiss, shutting her up and completely taking her breath away. His lips scorched hers, forcing her to remember vividly how it felt to be with, *really with,* Jack Dawson.

She had to stop this now. They weren't together any longer. She framed his face with her hands and urged him back. She homed in on his lips, his delicious sensual lips, which she wanted so badly to kiss again and again.

"Don't read too much into me visiting Chicago. That's why I never mentioned it. You didn't need to get the wrong idea—about us, I mean. It was for Ben, to see how you were. Nothing more. He was worried about you. You're his dad and were injured, and he was concerned and—"

"*Bunk*. You didn't even bring Ben with you." He tipped her face with his index finger—his touching her face an incredible turn-on—and brought her gaze to his. His eyes warmed to the color of rich prairie earth; his mood matched the tempest raging around them. His size dwarfed her, but she felt protected, cherished, *desired*.

More lightning cracked. The storm was nearly on top of them. Passion tightened Jack's face into hard lines, as the same feeling tore through her.

"Okay, so *I* was worried. Is that a crime?"

"How worried?" He kissed her hard. "This worried?" He said the words against her lips as he tightened her body to his. "Or this worried?" He kissed her as if the kiss were a brand and he was claiming her.

"Real worried," she finally managed to say. "Jack, this isn't a great idea. I can't get over you again."

But her protest was halfhearted and they both knew it. How could her brain insist she stay away from him, while her body insisted just the opposite? And how could her brain lose so easily? She was forty and smart. Brains were supposed to win at forty. Unless they had Jack Dawson to deal with.

His lips took hers again, hot, fierce, possessive, his strong hands bringing her body tighter still as his erection pressed into her belly. His kissing deepened, telegraphing his intention, making her hot. "I missed you. I missed this."

"Missed?" She could barely talk. "Try longed for, dreamed about, fantasized and salivated over."

His eyebrows arched a fraction, a tiny smile tipping the corners of his mouth. "No kidding?"

"What do you think?" She kissed him as she'd done a million times before, in reality and in her dreams. Dreams were a darn-poor replacement for the real thing. A familiar sensual pulse throbbed between her thighs. Her legs parted in anticipation and this time he was there to give her what she longed for. She was nothing but a forty-year-old wanton hussy! Okay, she could live with that!

His voice was low. "I want to make love to you."

"Oh, thank heavens. I'd hate to finish this alone."

He smiled, his eyes dancing. A chuckle slid up his throat.

"I'm trying to fight this, Jack, but I'm losing. Parting is hell, and then you leave and it starts all over again."

"It's no more hell than not being together at all. That's for damn sure." He cupped her bottom, his strong fingers pressing into her buttocks. She gasped. His eyes fired. "Sex with you is incredible—there's no denying that. But it will never be *just* sex between us, Maggie. We care too much. That's why you came to Chicago. That's why I fractured every bone in my body to find you today."

"I'm a mother of a college-bound student. Maybe…maybe I'm…too old for *this* sort of thing."

He slid his hands under her T-shirt and winked. "Let's find out."

"But…but…" She couldn't finish what she intended to say, and not just because he winked or because his mouth was on hers, but because those things together assaulted her senses. How could she put ideas together with Jack kissing her like this and her body wanting him so badly she ached?

His fingers trailed up her sides, making her skin quiver. He eased her bra over her breasts and her nipples hardened, waiting for his caress. He ran his fingers over her sensitive flesh, and she nearly melted into a blob right there on the porch.

She gasped for air, opening her mouth more to his invasion, taking his kiss deeper and deeper. She wound her fingers into the front of his damp shirt, but the desire to feel him everywhere drove her wild. She yanked the shirt out of his jeans and skimmed her hands over his bare back and tensed muscles. His warm skin under her fingertips was incredible; every inch of her begged for more. Oh, how she'd missed having him this near.

He nipped her left earlobe and planted a kiss behind it causing her to whimper. "We have the answer," he said.

"Answer?"

"Of you being too old."

Her hands roamed again over his sleek back, remembering, worshipping. Then over his incredible chest, the tight curls tickling her palms. "I'm not old." She looked at him. "Neither are you. You're—" she swallowed hard "—sexy as hell, Jack. You always were and nothing's changed."

"No, nothing has." He undid the snap and her jeans slid from her hips. The chill in the air washed over her thighs...*bigger now than thirteen years ago*...and her stomach...*not flat like thirteen years ago.* "Oh, no!"

Grabbing for the jeans, she jerked her head up, connecting hard with Jack's chin. He stumbled backward, staggered, then tripped, falling against the upright post. It creaked under the impact. He rubbed his chin and stared at her. "What the hell was that all about?"

Holding her jeans together in front with one protective hand, she smoothed back her hair with the other, trying to assume some degree of sophistication. "I'm not the same woman I was thirteen years ago."

"What's that supposed to mean?"

"I'm...rounder by about fifteen pounds."

His eyes scrunched in confusion.

"All right, I'm fatter. There, I said it. It's true. I'm not a size eight anymore. I'm a twelve or even a fourteen. I intended to lose ten pounds and at least be down to a size ten, but then Andy disappeared and Ben started dating that girl, and Dad and—"

"And you ate Snickers."

"I devoured Snickers, the perfect stress food, and now I have rounds where I should have flats and—"

He scooped her around the middle with one arm and held her up against the side of the building, his hot breath falling across her lips as his firm torso pressed into hers. "Listen to me, Maggie Moran once-upon-a-time Dawson, I don't give a flying fig what size you are. I don't care how old you are or what you wear or what you do to your hair or how sweet and sexy you smell every time you pass by me. I want to make love to *you*. I want to bury myself so deep inside you neither of us will ever forget this day."

He kissed her long and wet. "And the only way you're going to get me to stop making love to you is to say you don't want to. You don't want to as much as I want to."

He stepped away from the building and let her slip down against his very turned-on body, till her feet touched the floorboards. "It's your call, but do it quick. I only have so much control, Maggie. Make love to me here and now on this damn old porch in the middle of nowhere or I'm riding out of here into the storm, because being with you alone like this is more than I can take."

His eyes went to black. "And I can take pretty damn much."

He was gorgeous! So male, so virile, so much a hero many times over in spite of what it had cost him personally. *And he wanted her bad.*

How could she say no? She pushed him back so there wouldn't be any more head-to-chin incidents, yanked off one boot, then the other. She snatched the blanket and spread it out. Her eyes met Jack's and a devilish grin parted his lips as she eased her jeans and panties over her hips, down her legs to her toes, then kicked the rumpled heap to the side. "Now what?"

JACK FELT his chest tighten. The soft patch of dark curls between her legs entranced him. Her blouse fluttered in the wind, flattening the material against her torso, silhouetting her bare breasts underneath.

He couldn't have moved if he'd wanted to. Hell, for a moment nothing would bend. He'd been too long without her. He'd had other women over the years, but they weren't Maggie, *his Maggie.* He hungered to see all of her without clothes in the way, every delicious provocative inch he remembered so well.

"It's chilly out here, Jack."

"In a minute you won't notice, and neither will I." The rain had slacked to a drizzle, and the thunder headed over the plains. He unbuttoned her blouse, his fingers nearly numb with anticipation. The fact that he didn't rip the garment off was a real credit to his rapidly deteriorating self-control. He bared her shoulders and she unsnapped her bra, then let it drop to the floor. A joint effort. He smiled.

"What are you thinking that's making you so happy?"

"You. Naked. Standing right in front of me."

Her hair curled around her face, her breasts fine and full, her waist curved, her hips round and womanly. This had all happened in his dreams. But now was for real. Here Maggie was, in front of him. "You're…so beautiful."

"And you have clothes on." She stepped toward him, her body dancing a slow sexy sway. She undid his shirt…but not fast enough. He unfastened the buttons from the bottom up as she did them from the top down. "So many buttons, so much time already lost."

He yanked the shirt over his head, then he pulled off his boots and jeans.

He watched her eyes widen.

"Holy cow."

She was staring at him, and not into his eyes. He followed her gaze. Her eyes were focused on his erection. Maybe he wasn't...performing as well as he once did, though he sure felt he was, and then some.

"You're...bigger."

He gave her a cocky smile. "I bet we're still a perfect fit." His insides tightened at the desire blazing in her eyes. "You're just as I remembered, Maggie. Every single part of you drives me wild."

She picked up his jeans and fished out his wallet, took the condom from the back and turned it over in her hand. "Usual place, but it's kind of old, Jack." Her smile flashed wicked. "Good."

He laughed and put the condom on, then snatched her around the waist, his bare arm across her naked back driving home the fact that they were truly together. Then he eased her down onto the blanket and fixed himself over her, bracing with his other hand. He savored the feel of Maggie hot and wanting under him, finally, after so many years. "Do you know how many times I dreamed of us here like this?"

He kissed her neck, her chin, her nose, and she laughed, her face without stress, just as when they'd first met. Her legs wrapped around his middle. He clenched his jaw, searching for restraint, the thrill of them together almost too much to handle. His voice sounded hoarse as he said, "I've wanted this for so long I need to make it last."

"I don't think so, Jack. Not now." Her pupils dilated. She raised her head, capturing his mouth in a ravenous kiss, the feel of her arms and legs across his bare back reminding him of an incredible time in his life, a time when Maggie was a part of it.

"Jack?" She breathed his name on a husky sigh. "I've waited so long." She kissed him as his big plan to make love to her slowly, to savor every second, vanished like smoke into the night.

She arched her pelvis against him, inviting him, and in one thrust he was filling her, her gasps encouraging him, seducing him. His blood pounded, keeping pace with his body. Making love to Maggie was amazing, more powerful, more intense than ever. Did sex *improve* with age? *It sure as hell didn't deteriorate.*

She tightened her thighs more, her fingertips digging into his back. "Oh, Jack," she whimpered, her body tensing.

Then he felt her passion take uncontrollable possession of his and together they climaxed in a world all their own that they'd never forgotten.

He lay there for a moment, relishing being with Maggie. Cuddling her, cherishing her. He rested his forehead against hers, his breathing still raw. He looked into her blue eyes, glazed from their lovemaking, and brushed his lips across hers that was full and wet from his kisses. "How could we have ever let something like this go?"

"Too many things got in the way."

He ravished the sweetness of her delectable mouth.

"Uh-oh." He felt her body stiffen under him. "We have a problem."

He closed his eyes. "Can we for *once* not have a problem."

"Cars. Coming up the gravel driveway. I hear motors. The seniors joyriding again, no doubt." She pushed him over, sending him into a spread-eagled position on the floorboards.

"Here." She tossed him his clothes. The crumpled mass landed on his chest. "Uh…" He fished out her panties, silky and hot-pink, and twirled them on his finger. "A memento? For me?"

She snatched them from his finger. "They're not your size."

"Oh, I think we just proved they are."

"We'll laugh later. Right now we have to get out of here, unless you want us to be the primary source of gossip for the next year—make that years. The kids are as bad as the adults. Before night, you and I will have had wild sex at the depot, on horseback, in every barn and outbuilding and probably in the middle of town under a park bench. Exaggeration abounds."

"On horseback? Can you do that? Maybe we should find out."

"*No!* You get to go back to Chicago. I have to face these people and be a respectable rancher, not the town's floozy."

"The town's?" He arched his brow.

"Okay, Jack Dawson's."

He pushed himself to a standing position and yanked on his clothes, the last part of what Maggie said seeping into his brain. He was leaving and she wasn't. Once again, they'd be apart.

MAGGIE MOUNTED Cisco, the leather creaking as she pulled herself into the saddle. "We'll circle around behind the depot. The kids should be here any second and they won't see us. We can get lost in a stand of pine trees and take a different route home."

He nodded, saddled up, then flipped Butterfly's reins. "Go, horse."

"'Go, horse'? You got to be kidding." But to her amazement, Butterfly and rider took off, she and Cisco right beside them.

Jack bounced along in the saddle, his hat slipping to one side. Worst rider she'd ever seen, not a stick of rhythm in the man anywhere—*except when he made love to her.* He had all kinds of rhythm then, and just thinking about it made her nearly lose her balance and fall off Cisco.

"Hey." Jack caught her shoulder as they faded into the pines and slowed the horses to a walk. "Are you okay?"

She looked into Jack's eyes. Just having him here beside her was terrific. To talk to, laugh with, knowing it didn't matter to him if she did dumb things or not. They were way beyond the stage of impressing each other. Jack accepted her for who she was. No one else did that so completely. Mostly everyone expected something from her. Not Jack. She'd miss him when he left, *a lot.*

But there was no sense in dwelling on that now. "I think we made a clean getaway."

Sunlight flickering through the pines fell across Jack's shoulders. His hat cast shadows across his face, five-o'clock stubble darkened his chin. The only sound was the crunch of horse hooves on dry needles. It was a perfect time, a perfect setting; the perfect companion, except this time wouldn't last.

Somehow she had to distance herself from him. Put their relationship on a nonpersonal level. And she needed to start now and keep it up for the next eight days, *the longest eight days in the history of mankind,* so that when he left she wouldn't be a complete basket case the way she had been thirteen years ago. "When you ride, let your body acclimate to the movements of the horse."

Okay, that was good. Very nonpersonal.

He laughed. "This from the gal who nearly fell out of her own saddle?"

She tossed her head, giving him a superior smirk. "We'll just forget about that." She knew full well he would never forget and probably tease her forever, but only when the two of them were alone. "Think up down, up down. A steady cadence, a continuous beat. Think…"

Her eyes seized his and he arched his brow. "Sex?"

"I thought music."

His eyes turned the color of fine brandy. "You are such a bad liar."

She glanced away. Yeah, well, sometimes lying's justified. *Like now.* What had happened to nonpersonal?

She should find another topic. "What about you and Ben? Is our son still alive?"

Jack reined in Butterfly and leaned his forearm on the saddle horn, studying her from under the brim of his Stetson as she rode by. "Are you going to pretend we never made love, Maggie? That what happened at the depot wasn't meant to be and that we both didn't want it?"

She halted Cisco, turned and rode back to Jack. "I can live with that."

He frowned.

"All right, all right. I'm not going to pretend anything. It happened. Making love to you was great. You're always great, Jack. But it doesn't change anything between us, because we can't change who we are. If we keep thinking about making love to each other, how will we ever part and not go crazy? We have to let what happened at the depot go, and get on with our lives as before."

She touched his cheek. Not a great idea for someone who's just suggested they get on with their lives, but having him so close made him irresistible. She loved the feel of his rough skin against her fingers. His scent, which made her so aware of him any time they were together. She wanted to throw her arms around him, knocking them both to the ground, and make love all over again.

Instead, she sat up straight in the saddle. She should ride off into the sunset. Except, this wasn't sunset and she was no hero. She was Jack's horny ex-wife. "Tell me about Ben."

"This isn't going to work, you know."

"It will if we quit talking about it. *Tell me about Ben.*"

He sighed, then nudged Butterfly into a walk as they broke free of the stand of trees and out onto the open prairie.

Sun and silence hung in the air as they rode on, the last of the clouds now moving southwest to surprise the heck out of another unsuspecting couple who thought the storms were due tonight. Maybe that couple would make love at some old abandoned place. Maggie hoped so. And she hoped that couple had a more promising future than she and Jack did.

"Ben's fine," Jack finally said, snapping her back to the moment. "His parents are hopeless idiots who have no idea what the hell they're doing, but *he's* just fine. Mostly. I gave him one week to get his act together and tell us what was going on, before all hell breaks loose."

"Meaning you?"

Jack winked.

"Maybe I should—"

"Let me." Jack gave her a half smile that warmed her more than the sun. "I started this—I should finish it. Besides, you've spent enough time in parenthood hell and now…"

She reined in Cisco and stared at the ground. "My, my, what have we here?"

"What's wrong?" Jack stopped beside her.

"Wire cutters. Size large, industrial grade. The kind made for taking down barbed wire and padlocks."

Maggie slid to the ground and Jack followed. They hunkered over the cutters and he asked, "One of your hands?"

She shook her head as she picked the cutters up and turned them over. "We put our initials on everything. Most ranchers around here have some telltale marking so when we help one another out we all get our tools back. I doubt if there are any fingerprints. Folks use gloves for this kind of heavy work. No rust, so they haven't been out here that long."

Jack fingered the handle. "Fresh red paint. As if it dripped off something."

She gazed across the plains. "Too bad it rained. All the grass is matted from the downpour and there's no trail. I followed tire tracks from the cut in the fence to the depot. That's why I was there."

"Lucky you. I was dragged by a psycho horse." He pushed his hat to the back of his head. "What did you find at the depot?"

"The smaller tire tracks I followed got mixed up with larger tracks and then took off in another direction. Butch Anderson was the guy at the Purple Sage bad-mouthing my herd. He might have a medium-size truck like this, but then, most ranches around here do, so that's not much to go on."

"Think whoever did this met up with someone to sell off Andy?" She could barely get out the words and her stomach lurched.

"Were there buffalo prints in the dust at the depot? Any marshmallow remains scattered around?"

"With Andy there'd be no marshmallow remains. But I didn't see any hoofprints or matted patches of grass where a buffalo stomped. I guess they didn't off-load him." She let out a deep breath and crossed her fingers. "That's good news. Right?"

"Buys us time. I'd say whoever took Andy has him stashed somewhere and is waiting till he gets your calves. Then he'll sell them all off at once. The wire cutters and the cut fence you ran into the other night prove they're after more."

She stared at him and rolled her eyes. "Oh, thank you Mr. Optimist. I feel so much better now, thinking they haven't given up and are after the rest of my herd."

They stood and he draped his arm around her shoulders. "The bad guys dropped the wire cutters. They're getting sloppy, maybe desperate. Always a good sign. And we have some idea what's going on, except for the larger tracks. I don't know how they play into all this. Roy and I can catch your rustlers when they go after the calves. I'm sure it's the beefalo calves they're after, since they could have taken your regular beef cattle before now. Or maybe they'll get them next." He shrugged. "We have no way of knowing."

She slid from under his arm and gazed at him. "Roy? Excuse me!"

He chucked her under the chin and gave her a sappy-sweet grin that made him seem innocent, when all the while he was guilty as all get-out. "You've gotten this far, Maggie, and done a hell of a job. Now Roy and I can take over, along with your hands, and—"

"You're having a senior moment, right? You've forgotten that we already had this little conversation when you first got to Whistlers Bend. This is my bull and my ranch. Sound familiar?"

He put his hands to his hips, looking like he owned the earth. Chicago cop does Montana. "That was before things got this dangerous. I'm helping Roy now. It's the only thing to do."

She jammed her hands on her hips and tossed her head defiantly. "Roy can't. He's swamped already. And you can't even ride a horse. What kind of help is *that?*"

"A sore one." He swooped her into his arms. "But I'm strong and determined and mean as a tiger by the tail when provoked." He kissed her hard, making her furious at him for taking advantage of her like this, but more furious with herself because she really liked the kiss, even if it did come from the orneriest man west of the Mississippi. "This is not going to happen, Jack."

"Okay, then I'll go with you. We'll ride out together and hunt for Andy."

"And there will be more afternoons like the one at the depot. That can't happen. When you leave I'll be a mess. Once a mess is enough."

He sobered, his eyes dark with a hint of pain smoldering deep inside. "Yeah, it wasn't any picnic for me either when you left."

For a second neither of them said anything, both remembering a time that often seemed hell on earth. Then again, before they parted hadn't been any better, and they both knew it.

"You can get Henry to ride with you. I hear tell he can still shoot a fly off a donkey's butt at fifty yards. I'm not letting you go after rustlers alone."

"*Letting me?* As in I need your permission to do something? That'll be the day. And did you just say *hear tell* a moment ago?"

He took off his hat and raked a hand through his dark, full, lovely hair, which covered his very thick head. Before he could reply, she said, "Here's the deal, Jack. Roy has enough with being deputy and he has a family. Henry is out of the picture. I'd be too worried."

"And you think I wouldn't be?"

"I'm worried about his heart condition, not the situation. *I'm* going to spend the night with the calves and cows, then herd them down to the pastures behind the barns tomorrow so we can keep an eye on them, or at least do a better job than we are now. The hands will watch the rest of the herd in the mountains. That's the plan, and you'll have to deal with it."

"You can't go out all alone tonight, Maggie. It's too risky."

"I'll get BJ and Dixie to help."

Jack laughed—hard. She should be furious, except she nearly laughed, too. Where the heck had that idea about Dixie and BJ come from?

"A waitress and a doctor? Bet those rustlers will be shaking in their boots. Dixie and BJ probably know less than I do about cattle, and that's going some."

She squared her shoulders. "BJ, Dixie and I have lived here forever. We're all neighbors and friends and no one's going after us. This is a local job. We'll build a big fire and keep it going. The rustlers will take my cattle when no one is around, just as they ran off when my hands and I got too near last night. They're not after a confrontation, Jack. They're after ruining me the easiest way possible."

She climbed back on Cisco and watched Jack remount Butterfly. He turned in the saddle to face her. "I think you're right about whoever's after your stock avoiding a battle." A slow grin played at his mouth. "Besides, it'll be a real treat to see how BJ and Dixie react when you tell them they'll be spending the night huddled around a campfire, freezing their backsides off in the wide-open spaces of Montana."

"It'll be an adventure. They'll love it."

"Wanna bet?"

Chapter Six

BJ sat up ramrod straight in the booth at the Purple Sage and glanced around as if she suspected Maggie must be talking to someone else, not her. She exchanged looks with Dixie, whose carafe of coffee was poised midair as she stood there, frozen in astonishment. Finally, BJ managed to say, "You want *us*—as in Dixie and me, the original town girls, to go with *you* to hunt rustlers—" she pointed to the window "—out *there?*"

"Well, we can't do it from in here. It's a cow-rescue operation. Whoever took Andy is also after my breeding cattle and new calves, I realize that now."

Dixie rolled her shoulders. "Great, we'll be sitting ducks."

"This isn't a 'shoot it out at high noon' thing. It's a 'let's torment Maggie till she gives up' thing. As long as there's someone around, the bad guys stay away. We'll have a huge fire, and move the cattle to the pastures behind the barn tomorrow. Dad will ride out and help me herd. You just come with me and spend the night."

Maggie slid from the purple-cushioned booth and retrieved the coffee carafe from Dixie, who still hadn't moved. She filled a waiting patron's cup, nudged Dixie into the spot just vacated and turned over an ever-present white cup on saucer. Then she poured coffee for Dixie and topped off BJ's. A little pampering went a long way in situations like this.

BJ absently added cream, a dumbfounded look still clouding her face. "Why can't you send out your hands? That's what you pay them for. I do not sleep with cattle." She cleared her throat and tipped her head. "Well, except for Randall Cramer, ex-fiancé and undoubtedly still the biggest jackass on the face of the earth."

Maggie broke a piece of doughnut from Dixie's plate. "Technically, jackasses aren't cattle, but we get the point. And my hands are in the mountains, checking on the rest of the herd. Think of it this way—the three of us haven't spent the night together in a long time. We need fun, some excitement. An experience. This is it."

BJ snatched another chunk of Dixie's doughnut. "'Fun' is the year-end clearance at Pretty in Pink. 'Exciting' is new lingerie at the Peek-a-Boo Boutique. As for an 'experience,' I vote for the Bellagio in Vegas or the Carlisle in New York. Both are a great experience."

"I'm talking fun like when we were kids. Carefree summer days. Camp."

Dixie swatted at BJ's hand as she made for the last bit of pastry. "I hated camp. Don't you remember how we all griped for the whole two weeks we were there every year? The closest I've gotten to camping the past twenty-five years is the L.L. Bean catalog."

Maggie swept her hand through the air. "Think about sleeping under the open skies, stars overhead, fresh air, gentle breezes—"

"Dirt in my hair, bugs in my sleeping bag. Snakes. Omigod, snakes." Dixie sucked air in through gritted teeth, followed by some whiny sound that drew the attention of every patron in the Purple Sage. "I hate bugs and snakes. When was the last time I called you to kill a bug for me?"

"Last week. And this time I'll be right there to squash the little suckers flat."

BJ shook her head. "I'm the doctor around here. I can't just pick up and leave."

"Doc LaMar over in Rocky Fork can cover for you. Heaven knows you fill in for him often enough when he goes skiing and golfing."

BJ nibbled her lower lip. "I have red hair, freckles. I get sunburned and my nose swells and peels and looks like a fried onion."

"It'll be at night. The most you'll have to worry about is moon burn."

Maggie refilled her own cup. This was not going well, even for a one-night outing. She had to level with them. Well, sort of.

She folded her hands on top of the table. "Okay, here's the deal. Now that Jack's landed in Whistlers Bend and seems to be making himself right at home, he won't hesitate to return if I don't show him I can handle things. He'll fly back every time he believes I have any kind of problem, and completely take over my life, *again,* even though he lives in Chicago."

BJ gave Maggie a hard look. "And?"

Maggie raised both hands, palms up. "Good grief. Isn't that enough? Consider another doctor running your practice. I don't need someone telling me what to do. I love my independence and running the ranch, and Jack Dawson will not back off unless I can prove to him he's not my salvation. If I don't take a stand now, I'm doomed."

Dixie rolled her shoulders seductively. "Honey, from what I've seen, having Jack around isn't exactly a hardship."

Maggie felt a blush creep into her cheeks as she considered her and Jack together. The man was many things, but Dixie was right—hardship wasn't one of them.

BJ said, "So bring Jack with you tonight into the wilds of Montana. He'll find out how capable you are and not have to interfere ever again."

Maggie puffed out a lungful of air. "Being alone with Jack under a full moon and starry sky isn't exactly in his or my best interest." She fiddled with a napkin. "Heck, a torrential downpour wasn't even in our best interest."

Dixie stared at Maggie for a moment without saying anything. "You didn't."

BJ gasped and stage-whispered to Dixie. "That's it. She did. *They* did. Omigosh."

Maggie's blush deepened. She could feel the heat in her cheeks. How could this happen at forty? Wasn't there some expiration date on blushing, when it just went inactive? "When Jack leaves I don't want to be attached to him all over again—at least, not any more than I already am."

"Am!" Dixie's eyes widened.

Oh, drat! "Forget *am*. I could ask Roy to go with me, but he's busy here in town, and Jack's not about to let me go alone. I want him to know I can handle it—*we* can handle it without his expert advice. That if I have a problem I can rely on you two." She looked from one to the other. "I'll bring s'mores. We all love s'mores."

Dixie stood, retrieved the coffee carafe and poured coffee for two customers without even looking their way. She pulled herself up to all her five feet, three inches and straightened her lavender apron over her well-rounded figure. "The good part of being forty is a refined sense of taste. Forget s'mores. Throw in champagne and caviar and it's a deal, and only because you're my friend and not because I agree with you."

"I have to bribe you?"

Dixie tsked. "Well, of course. We'll spend the night where the buffalo roam and antelopes play." She narrowed her eyes at Maggie. "Do you think antelopes really play?"

BJ patted her lips with her paper napkin, refolded it and placed it beside her coffee cup. Finishing-school manners at the local café. She glanced at Maggie. "I need to straighten out a few things before I go. We'll meet you at Sky Notch about seven? I'll pick up strawberries. Champagne without strawberries is a sin."

Champagne, caviar and strawberries weren't exactly

on the official cowboy menu, but if they worked, what the heck. "Let's make it six. I'll send Jack on errands in town so he doesn't follow us."

Dixie eyed her. "That man would follow you to the ends of the earth. Isn't it romantic?"

"Try overprotective and controlling. It's a cop thing, especially with Jack. If there's a bad guy out there, he's got to nab him. It's in his blood—comes from his father and grandfather. You guys are saving me."

Three hours later, as Maggie studied BJ and Dixie—complete with new white Stetson—both women mounted up and waiting outside the barn, Maggie was confident her plan would work. She patted the bags on the packhorse. "I've got fixings for chuck-wagon stew."

"What happened to champagne, caviar and strawberries?" Jack asked as she led Butterfly from the barn.

Maggie glanced at BJ, who seemed as dumbfounded as she felt to see Jack there. Then Maggie looked at Dixie, who didn't seem surprised to see Jack at all. Maggie turned to Jack. "New hat?"

He rolled his eyes upward toward the brim. "Couldn't borrow Henry's forever." He nodded at BJ and Dixie. "You ladies don't mind if I tag along, do you?"

Maggie folded her arms. "You should stay here, play chess with Dad and help Ben with calculus."

"Your dad's with Irene and my folks. Ben understands calculus better than I ever did." He flashed Dixie and BJ his most winning smile. "I have great cop stories for around the campfire."

Maggie groused, "This is Jack Dawson's way of saying, 'If you think I'm letting three women ride out of here alone into the night with cattle rustlers on the loose, you're crazy as hell.'"

"There is that." Jack grinned.

He had a terrific grin, the kind any woman would fall for, especially the two on horseback *and* the one standing on the ground, fuming. "The deal was I not ride out alone. We had this little conversation before." She pointed to BJ and Dixie. "See, not alone."

Dixie readjusted her hat. "Just for the record, BJ and I have no opinion on this one way or the other. That's what best friends do—butt out. We're very good at butting out."

Maggie wrinkled her nose. "Is that what you said when you ran into Jack while shopping for your Stetson?"

"We might have talked a little." Dixie flipped the horse's reins and headed for the prairie, *away* from Maggie's accusations.

BJ tagged along as Maggie called, "Follow the creek bed east. I'll catch up." She faced Jack, totally irresistible in well-worn jeans, soft denim shirt and a hint of a tan. *Be strong! Resist!* "You're not coming, Jack. I got this covered. We'll be fine. I've been fine for thirteen years. That's not going to change."

"With all that's going on right now, a cop around wouldn't be the end of the world."

She readjusted her own Stetson. "You being around isn't the end of the world, but it sure complicates the heck out of life as I know it. You can't come running every time I have a problem. I have to live my life my way."

"The key word here is *live*."

Dixie yelled over her shoulder, "How much longer? I think I have to go to the bathroom. Did anyone pack toilet paper? My new boots are rubbing a blister. Will my cell phone work where we're going? It's too hot."

Maggie closed her eyes and massaged her forehead. Jack chuckled. "Welcome to the trip from hell."

She peeked up at him. "You're enjoying this, aren't you?"

He nodded. "You got yourself into this one, Maggie girl. Good luck." Then the expression in his eyes turned serious. "Build a huge fire and be safe."

JACK SAT at the kitchen table, drank his coffee and watched Ben head upstairs to his room. He'd come straight home after baseball practice, eaten, then helped Jack clean up the dishes. Ben seemed okay, but Jack could tell something was bothering him. *That girl.*

Hell! When a man was bothered, *that girl* was always mixed up in it some way.

But who was she? Where did she live? What kind of parents did she have? Jack's coffee suddenly tasted sour, and heartburn set his chest on fire. Kid worries sucked, especially when coupled with ex-wife worries.

He brought his mug to the sink and dumped it, then stared out the window. A pink-blue-and-purple sunset blazed across the sky from the Beartooth Mountains to the Pryor Mountains. "Incredible."

"It's the reward we get for living through the winters of the damned out here," Henry said from behind.

Jack turned. "Thought you were out with Irene and Edward and Gert and having dinner in Rocky Fork?"

"So did I." Henry raked his hand over his head, standing thin wisps of gray on end. "Irene had to wash her hair. Or was it clean her closet? Whatever, it was a damn poor excuse. I sent your parents on. Kind of lost the fun when Irene pooped out on me. I don't know what's wrong between us all of a sudden. Things were fine and dandy, and tonight…" He shook his head.

"Did you try to tell her what to do? That seems to be getting me in a boatload of trouble these days."

"Irene lives with her daughter and son-in-law. They're not too keen about her spending so much time with me. I bet they're afraid we're getting sweet on each other, and they're convincing her that us being together isn't a good thing. Me spending the night on the couch didn't sit well with them at all."

"*Are* you sweet on her?"

Henry swiped his head again. "I'm sixty-five, Jack. Irene's fifty-five. When you've had a triple bypass that's a big ten years."

Jack retrieved a bottle of juice from the fridge and put it in Henry's hand as he said, "I'm no spring chicken."

He reclaimed the chair he'd vacated, as Henry took the one on the other side. "And I haven't seen your name in the obituary column of the newspaper, either. None of us has any guarantees on life. That's one thing being a cop teaches you real fast."

"Yeah, but those kids think that there's no one like

their daddy, and their mama should be content to live with the memory. Then there's the fact that Irene's a townie. Living out here in the middle of nowhere isn't her cup of tea." Henry took a swig of juice and made a face at it. "Damn poor substitute for a long-neck."

"Yeah, and being alone is a damn poor substitute for being with someone you care about." Jack traced the wood grain on the tabletop with his index finger. "Maggie and I've spent the past thirteen years apart, Henry. I miss her. Miss her like mad every single day. I have no one to blame except myself. I can live with that. But I'll be damned if I'll ever let someone else put me in that situation. To live apart was our decision, no one else's. This is between you and Irene. It's your lives, and to hell with anyone who tries to interfere. No one has that right." He eyed Henry. "Ever think about selling the ranch and moving into town?"

Henry shook his head. "Sell Sky Notch? What would I do? What would Maggie do?"

"Rustlers, beefalo, constant work—not a pretty picture for a town girl like Irene, and damn dangerous for Maggie. Maybe if you and Irene compromised, you'd find some middle ground and—"

The back door banged open, framing Dixie and BJ against the setting sun. Jack glanced from one to the other as Dixie held out her left arm. "Spider bite. It hurt something awful and looked dangerous so BJ thought we better head on back."

Henry walked over to Dixie. "How bad is it?" He studied her outstretched arm. "I don't see anyth—"

"Oh." She dropped her left arm and stuck out her

right one. "There." She pointed to a red spot. "I should rest. Maggie didn't leave any of that champagne behind, did she? Bet I could rest just fine with a glass of champagne in my hand."

"I'm thinking mosquito bite," offered Henry as he squinted at the redness.

Dixie yanked her arm away. "Spider. Definitely spider." She cradled her arm as though it might fall off at any moment.

BJ said, "We had to leave poor Maggie all alone out there in the wilderness with her cows and calves and champagne chilling in the creek and fresh strawberries and caviar. All alone. What a pity."

"And," added Dixie, "what if those big bad rustlers return? Who's going to protect—"

"Maggie bought this load of bullhonkey?" Jack said, folding his arms.

BJ tipped her chin. "I'm a doctor." She poked herself in the chest with her finger and tried for sincere expression, except Barbara Jean Fairmont couldn't lie for beans. "Maggie always believes my load of bullhonkey. Uh, not that this is a load of bull."

BJ turned as red as Dixie's fingernail polish. "What I mean is… Oh, for heaven's sake, Jack, just go out and help her. It's dangerous."

Henry slapped Jack on the back. "You're not up to more time in the saddle, boy. I can go help Maggie tonight. Spent many a night sleeping with the herd and—"

"*No!*" Dixie and BJ said together. They exchanged looks as a guilty silence filled the room.

Dixie finally let out a big sigh and removed her hat. "Okay, okay. You caught us. Maggie sent us here to get Jack to go be with her. She wants him."

"Bad," added BJ. "There's the moon, the stars, the wide-open spaces and champagne. You get the picture. She didn't want to seem desperate. An ex never wants to seem desperate—not that Maggie *is* desperate. Anyway, she reconsidered and cooked up this little scheme of the spider."

Jack folded his arms. "Right."

"It's the truth." Dixie huffed. "Maggie misses you, she wants you."

Jack gave BJ his best cop stare, guaranteed to make anyone sweat in thirty seconds. She swallowed and squirmed, then said, "Maggie's missed you for thirteen years, Jack, and that's the gospel truth, I swear."

She swallowed again, took Dixie by the sleeve and dragged her toward the door. "We have to go. I have patients."

Dixie added, "You better hurry, Jack, while you still have the light. Just follow the creek. Maggie's camped right beside it. You can't miss her. She's waiting for you and she's out there all alone."

Jack watched the dynamic duo scurry out the back door, then he said to Henry, "You think Abbott and Costello are telling the truth?"

Henry laughed. "Which part? But Maggie would never buy into that spider-bite story any more than we have. Still, I'm thinking she's got to be in on this some way."

Jack stared out the window. "She wants to be with me?"

Henry shrugged. "What other answer is there? The two girls are here and Maggie's not." He laughed. "We both got woman business to tend to tonight and we better get a move on. I got a feeling tonight's going to be real interesting for both of us."

"You're going after Irene?"

"You bet. Time's a wasting, just like you said." He winked and walked away, and Jack took off for the barn. Before he left Whistlers Bend he'd probably be pretty good at saddling a horse; now, if he could only learn to ride one. He led Butterfly out of the barn, mounted and made for the creek. He headed east, trying to ignore the stabbing pains that plagued every inch of his abused body.

Well, not *every* inch. His eyelids were okay and his left elbow didn't hurt too much, but everywhere else felt as though he were a walking voodoo doll.

A half sun hovered on the mountain peaks, before taking the final plunge below. The air stilled and cooled, encouraging him to button up his jacket. He had to get a move on or he'd never find Maggie in the dark. He'd be damn lucky to find her in daylight.

And he really, really needed to find her. Not only shouldn't she be out there alone with someone after her cattle, but he wanted to be with her again. And if even half of what BJ and Dixie said was true, Maggie wanted him, too. He started to grin, but agony made him grit his teeth, instead. When he got back to Chicago he'd treat his Jeep to a tank of high-test and kiss the hood.

The sun dipped lower, and forty minutes later Jack's hope of finding Maggie vanished along with the daylight…until he heard a low mooing drift his way. He rounded a bend in the creek and spied a campfire glowing against the black sky. *Well, dogies.*

No! No dogies. Chicago cops did not say *dogies.* They used street slang mixed with swear words that turned the air blue. Somehow, though, that didn't fit out here. "Maggie?" he called into the night.

He heard a rifle cock. "*Holy cow!* It's me, Jack. Put your weapon down, girl."

As he drew closer he spotted her fine silhouette, which he'd know anywhere. Rifle cradled in her arms, she was like a pioneer woman, protecting what was hers. Maggie had the same spirit, the commitment, the determination and guts. "You should have made sure it was me before you disarmed."

"No one in Whistlers Bend calls a rifle a *weapon* or me *girl.* What the heck are you doing here?"

He drew up next to her, pushed his Stetson to the back of his head and gazed down at her in the firelight. He winked. "Miss me?"

"I just saw you a couple hours ago."

He gave her a devilish chuckle as he slid from the saddle. He wrapped the reins around a branch. "You can drop the pretense of not knowing what I'm doing here. Your plan worked. I came."

He bent his head and kissed her, letting his lips trail over hers, taking in the full sensual feel of her mouth.

"That's very nice," she said against his lips, her voice ragged, her eyes bright, reflecting the early moonlight. "But what do you mean by *pretense?*"

"Of not knowing why or how I got here." He kissed her again, stepping close, letting the heat from her body flow into his and loving every second of it. His erection pushed against the confines of his jeans. "I appreciate that you don't want to stay away from me even for one night."

Maggie broke the kiss, his lips and tongue suddenly making out with thin air. She stepped back. "Where did this great idea suddenly spring from?"

"The spider story." He grinned more, snaked his arms around her back and brought her to him in one motion. "Why else would you go along with that crazy tale unless you wanted me here with you?"

"I told you to stay at the ranch. And a spider bite can be dangerous."

"Not if it looks like a mosquito bite. You sent BJ and Dixie to get me. Hell, I'm flattered."

Her eyes widened. "Wait a minute. You think I tricked you into riding out here? That I'm *flattering* you? That I can't live without you and that you're *irresistible?*"

"Sounds about right. Except for the *irresistible*. That might be a stretch, but—"

"You conceited jerk." She pushed at his chest, sending him stumbling backward. Her eyes widened and she grabbed for him, missed as he tripped over a rock, then fell butt first into the creek, splashing water everywhere and drenching him from his new hat to his boots.

He closed his eyes as cold water crept into every pore of his body. *"Well, damn."*

Her eyes covered half her face. "Are you all right?"

"You couldn't live in hot-springs Arizona, could you? It had to be ice-water Montana."

She made her way to the edge of the creek, balanced herself on a rock and held out her hand. "Guess I shouldn't have pushed so hard."

"Yeah, and I shouldn't have tugged so hard." He captured her hand and toppled her into in the creek. As he grabbed her around the waist to break her fall, she landed right beside him.

She spluttered, her eyes furious. *"Why did you do that?"*

"I'm pissed. You get me all the way out here with your little scheme, then you don't want me here at all. Hell, I've got a right to be pissed. You keep changing your mind. How the hell am I supposed to know what you want?"

"I'm not changing anything and there is no scheme."

"That spider-bite story. Why would you go along with it unless you planned for BJ and Dixie to get me and—"

"I never saw the bite. They wrote me a note. I was tagging strays, and when I got back they'd already left." She stood, dripping water like a fountain. She glared down at him. "Whatever happed is their doing. *Not mine.*"

"A note? We were both set up." He stood, feeling like a human sponge and a big dumb-ass. She got his hat and dumped out the water.

"And now we're wet and freezing. Thought you could spot a con a mile away." She sloshed her way up the bank. "What happened?"

"Ego." He followed her, slowly, his boots weighing

in at about five hundred pounds by now. "My big fat ego. We have to get out of these clothes."

She gave him a you-did-this-on-purpose stare.

"Hey, you pushed me, remember?"

"And you pulled me."

"Seemed like a justifiable reaction at the time. Sorry." He unwound the reins from the branch and led Butterfly toward the fire, trailing squishy sounds and what sure sounded like horse laughter. He watched Maggie tug clothes from a saddlebag.

"You have something dry?"

"You don't?"

"I thought I was coming here to take clothes *off*."

She laughed and tossed him a blanket. "I have stew."

"And you're willing to share?"

"And when we get back home we'll have a roast—BJ's and Dixie's meddlesome hides. How could they do this to us?"

Shivers ran up Jack's back as he yanked off his wet clothes to spread by the fire. He knew Maggie was doing the same thing. He loved her undressing, revealing herself to him little by little. Memory mixed with longing and settled in his lower regions. No amount of cold diminished his desire for her. Not that it was going to do him one speck of good tonight.

He wrapped himself in the blanket and shuffled his way over to the fire. He should dry off, chase away the cold *and* forget about Maggie in the buff. *Yeah, like that was going to happen with her thirty feet away.*

She drew up beside him, dressed in jeans and an old

soft sweatshirt. She ladled stew onto a plate and passed it to him. "Sit down and eat. I have bread warming on a rock." She nodded toward the fire. "You're tired and cold. I don't need you croaking on me out here. Burying your sorry remains in this rocky dirt would be no picnic."

"Wouldn't dream of inconveniencing you."

"Darn right." She handed him a cup and he took a long drink. "Champagne?"

"Neither of us is big on fish eggs, but the strawberries look pretty good."

He sat down by the fire as the last of the night enfolded them. "I'm sorry about all this, Maggie. I made myself believe you wanted me as much as I want you."

She studied him for a long moment. "Good grief, Jack. I do want you. I wasn't exactly an uninvolved partner at the depot."

"Yeah, but I'm not as important to you as the ranch."

"And you're willing to give up being a cop for me, right?" The embers spat and cracked and sent sparks dancing into the air. "I like running the ranch, developing the new herd. You're a respected detective. We have to be who we are apart or we'll end up hating each other together."

The stew lodged in his throat and he washed it down with the champagne. He poured a splash more and clinked his cup with Maggie's.

"To us?"

"Yeah, two of the most stubborn, independent people on the planet, who just happened to fall in love.

Get FREE BOOKS and a FREE GIFT when you play the...

LAS VEGAS
GAME

Just scratch off the gold box with a coin. Then check below to see the gifts you get!

YES! I have scratched off the gold box. Please send me my **2 FREE BOOKS** and **gift for which I qualify.** I understand that I am under no obligation to purchase any books as explained on the back of this card.

354 HDL D7ZU   154 HDL D7YL

FIRST NAME

LAST NAME

ADDRESS

APT.#

CITY

STATE/PROV.

ZIP/POSTAL CODE

(H-AR-08/05)

7	7	7	Worth TWO FREE BOOKS plus a BONUS Mystery Gift!
🍒	🍒	🍒	Worth TWO FREE BOOKS!
🔔	🔔	♣	TRY AGAIN!

www.eHarlequin.com

Offer limited to one per household and not valid to current Harlequin American Romance® subscribers. All orders subject to approval.

BUSINESS REPLY MAIL
FIRST-CLASS MAIL   PERMIT NO. 717-003   BUFFALO, NY

POSTAGE WILL BE PAID BY ADDRESSEE

HARLEQUIN READER SERVICE
3010 WALDEN AVE
PO BOX 1867
BUFFALO NY 14240-9952

NO POSTAGE
NECESSARY
IF MAILED
IN THE
UNITED STATES

How the heck did we ever get together in the first place?"

He shrugged and sipped the champagne. "We don't have any choice who we fall in love with. And that's too damn bad."

He downed the rest of the wine in one gulp and finished his stew in two bites. "Think I'll sleep. We have a big day tomorrow moving the cattle back to Sky Notch."

MAGGIE WASN'T SURE how long she gazed at the fire, listening to Jack's heavy breathing, until she finally fell asleep…only to be awakened by Jack's hand over her mouth as he looked into her eyes. He put his finger across his lips in a be-quiet gesture and whispered in her ear, "We have company."

She felt her eyes widen as the rumble of a truck engine drifted their way. She glanced at the fire. Dead out. They should have taken turns keeping it going. He let go of her mouth and she mouthed, "Where's my rifle?"

He ignored her question and pointed over the outcrop of rocks. "There are three men. They might be armed."

"So am I!"

She tried to get up, but he stopped her, put his hand back over her mouth and shook his head. *What! He intended to let these jerks have her cows, her calves? Was he out of his ever-loving mind?*

She struggled against him and he tightened his grip, wrapping his body around hers to still her thrashing. Normally, this could be a good thing. Totally enjoyable. *But not now!* How could he let those vile people take her cattle? She jabbed him with an elbow to the ribs, but he didn't move a muscle, just grunted.

Mooing filled the air again, she could hear the herd stomping around, agitated. *Damn the rustlers. Damn Jack.*

Minutes passed—or was it hours?—and then the truck headed away. She fought to stand, and this time Jack let her go.

She jumped up and faced him, using every ounce of control not to pick up a stick and beat him with it. "What are you doing? We had the rustlers right here. Right where we are and did nothing."

"And what if they had guns?"

She spread her arms wide and toed the rifle beside her. "This isn't a slingshot. You let them take my cattle. I'm going to lose everything at this rate."

"Not your life."

She kicked a rock across the ground. "*Damnation.* Go back to Chicago, where you belong, and let me live my own life. Just…get out of here. It'll be light soon. You won't get lost."

"I'm not leaving you with a herd—"

"Herd?" She waved her arm across the prairie. "What's left of it."

"You can't bring it in by yourself."

Her gaze fused with his.

"I'll send out Henry." He jammed his hands on his hips. "If you're too thickheaded to see this was an explosive situation that could have ended badly, that's your damn problem, not mine."

"They're going to sell my cows. That's my problem."

"Not if we get a bulletin out on what's going on and everyone's on the lookout for beefalo calves and Andy. Your animals are like rare diamonds. Hard to get rid of without raising an eyebrow or two along the way."

"What if they take them somewhere far away by truck? Huh? Answer me that?" She ran her fingers through her hair in frustration as he snatched up his hat.

"They won't do that right after they nab them. They're holding them somewhere and will probably come back for the rest. They think they're getting away with it."

"Hey, I got news for you, they are! And when they return you'll probably help herd the cattle together for them and tie pretty bows on their tails."

He muttered swearwords as he faded into the darkness. She fished her flashlight from the saddlebags and scanned the beam across the herd. It was hard to tell just how many remained, but the truck hadn't sounded all that big and the rustling hadn't lasted all that long. Why hadn't they used the bigger truck? Unless that truck wasn't theirs, which begged the question, whose was it? And how in blazes did the rustlers know where the herd was in the first place?

She sighed and massaged her forehead as the first touch of dawn inched over the mountaintops, turning the world dusky-gray. She watched Jack ride out into the morning fog without so much as goodbye.

Well, fine. So, he was pissed. She was double pissed. But at least, added a little voice in her head she'd rather not listen to, she was alive to feel that way.

Chapter Seven

Six hours later as Maggie walked into the Purple Sage she wasn't all that sure about the *alive* part. She'd feel even worse if Henry hadn't helped her bring in the herd.

At thirty she'd been able to herd cattle and do chores and take care of Ben and consider all her responsibilities just part of the day. At thirty she'd had a flat stomach that would look much better under this new blue silk skirt. At thirty the ranch was still run by her dad, things were *his* way and the prospect of being bought out by the conglomerates seemed inevitable.

Maggie smiled to herself; not *everything* about being *forty* sucked.

"Yoo-hoo, Maggie," Dixie called from their usual window booth, the one they had used since high school. She and BJ grinned and waved as if they hadn't seen her in years. Maggie headed in their direction, avoiding the lemon meringue pie chilling in the display case, and sat down beside Dixie as she gushed, "Terrific skirt. Isn't that a terrific skirt, BJ?"

"And I love the sandals. You have a fantastic tan." BJ

faced Dixie. "Doesn't she have a fantastic tan? And new earrings? Where'd you get them?"

Maggie leaned an elbow on the table and rested her chin in her palm. "You gave them to me for Christmas."

Dixie rummaged around in her purse and pulled out the little silver flask she carried for medicinal purposes, and any other gritty purposes that warranted brandy. Then she stood, got the coffee carafe, poured Maggie coffee and added a splash of brandy.

Maggie eyed Dixie. "What's that for?"

"Mellow you out a bit. We want you a little mellow so we can explain what we did yesterday and you don't have a conniption fit—"

Dixie said, "Look, we had no idea things would turn out the way they did. All we meant was for you and Jack to be alone together to fix your problems. You're a great couple. We want you back that way. And that really *is* a terrific skirt."

Maggie ran her hand over the smooth silk. "Wait till you see the hunter-green blouse I bought. And why are you so sure things didn't work out with Jack and me?"

Dixie pursed her lips. "We don't. Not exactly. More like an educated guess. One of your hands, Lucky Thomas, rode into the ranch at dawn and ran into Jack. Actually, he heard Jack before he saw him, cussing and grumbling enough to raise the dead."

BJ stirred her coffee. "Not exactly afterglow from an evening in paradise."

"How'd Lucky get into the mix?"

Dixie tipped her chin. "See? That's what happens

when you get too busy. You start missing all the good gossip—unless you work at the Purple Sage here." She swept her hand over the diner. "Gossip central. Lucky's going with one of our cooks and he stopped in for breakfast."

BJ put in an order for a bagel and cream cheese and Maggie gazed at her two best friends, who'd been with her through everything life had to offer and then some. "Okay, things last night weren't exactly great, but I suppose they could have ended a whole lot worse than they did."

Dixie studied her mosquito bite. "You're telling me! I could have *really* been bitten by a spider. I hate spiders."

"Even worse than rustlers?" Maggie gripped her hands as they began to shake. "They dropped in for a little visit right before dawn."

BJ gasped and Dixie said, "Oh, my gosh. And we missed it. You and Jack got them, right? Nailed their ornery carcasses to the jailhouse wall! We didn't hear about that part. Did you find Andy?"

"Jack and I were outnumbered and Jack would have no part of me charging in like the D-Day invasion. Which is exactly what I would have done if the three of us had been out there alone and…"

She felt sick as Dixie beamed and said, "Then *we* would have captured the rustlers. We'd be town heroes."

Maggie and BJ looked at her as if she'd lost her mind. And Dixie added, "Or not. Guess that is a little over the top. But everyone's alive and well and drinking spiked coffee. So, what's the problem with you and Jack?"

Maggie's hand shook and she put down the coffee cup. She swallowed hard. "The problem is what *could* have happened if it had been the three of us instead of me and Jack. If we had been the ones to let the fire burn out."

BJ patted her arm. "But everything's fine. Just like that time when I jumped off the old railroad trestle and you both dove in the river to save me and we all nearly drowned but didn't."

"Then we signed you up for swimming lessons," Dixie added. "You still can't swim worth a hoot." She said to Maggie, "I understand what happened with the rustlers—you wanted to get them, Jack thought it better to see the next sunrise. But what happened between you and Jack that put him in such a pissy mood?"

"I was a dope."

"You already established that." Dixie spread her hands wide in frustration. "Spit it out."

Maggie hunched over her coffee. "I told Jack to go back to Chicago and quit making decisions for me."

"Oh, crap." Dixie drank straight from the flask. "You didn't."

BJ took a drink of Maggie's coffee. "There goes one romance shot straight to heck. How can you let a perfectly wonderful man escape like that?"

"He's not wonderful—at least, not all the time. Like when he's trying to run my life, which he was trying to do then."

"Maybe Dixie and I could help—"

"*No!* Jack is going away no matter what happens between us, and that's the way it should be, but I do owe him an apology." She sighed. "A really big apology for being…"

"A pain in the ass." Dixie winked.

"I was thinking irrational, but I'm sure he'd like your description better. The one thing I still don't understand is how in the heck the rustlers knew where the herd was to begin with. It's like they drove right to us, loaded cattle and left. A planned event."

Eyes bugged, Dixie stared straight ahead, not breathing as Maggie said, "What did you do? Call them up and draw them a map?"

"Not…intentionally." Dixie bit at her lower lip. "After we got home last night I went to the Cut Loose to show off my hat and hear the new group who were playing. Jack's parents were there and had a great time and—"

"Dixie!" Maggie hissed.

"All right. All right. I started talking to Ray. He was tending bar and I sort of mentioned I'd been out tending the herd with you on East Fork Creek—thought that sounded kind of impressive. I showed him the new Stetson I bought for going on my first cattle drive and told him we'd come back early and it wasn't that far away, which was good, because I hadn't been on a horse for a really long time and…well, you get the general idea."

"And the bar was packed, I suppose?"

Dixie huffed. "With the new group in town, of course the place was packed. Everyone loved my hat and I had to keep repeating my story about why I bought it. I wasn't thinking about rustlers being there, just country-western music and doing the Montana two-step and having fun." She winked. "Which I did big-time."

Maggie drummed her fingers. "All of which reinforces the idea that the rustlers are local—as Jack said—*and* they visit the Cut Loose."

"And," added Dixie, "they're people who have fine taste in music and appreciate sexy hats."

Maggie wagged her head. "I better tell Roy what's going on and then…then I'll head back to the ranch."

"To apologize to Jack?" Dixie nodded at the lemon meringue pie in the case. "Buy it. You don't have time to make one of your own. You need to soften him up."

Maggie sighed. "There may not be that many lemon meringue pies in all of Montana."

Maggie kicked off her sandals as she entered the kitchen. She put the pie in the fridge and started to warm the spaghetti sauce sitting on the stove. She stopped and stared. Had she made spaghetti sauce before going into town? She gazed out the kitchen window to the mountains turning purple in the late-afternoon sunlight, and a sense of peace hung in the air the way it always did at this time of day.

Things weren't perfect, but thanks to Jack Dawson and his levelheaded approach to the rustler situation, they were one heck of a lot better than they might have been.

The minivan wasn't there when she'd arrived and neither was Henry's Mustang, so Jack must be off somewhere. *Good.* She needed to figure out what to say before he showed up. Driving home hadn't inspired her. Neither did stirring spaghetti sauce now or looking out the window. Maybe doing laundry would. The idea of *coming clean* might spark something in the way of an apology—if she could find the darn laundry basket.

First the sauce, now the laundry. The day was a blur, her brain oatmeal. Did that happen to forty-year-old brains?

She checked Henry's room for the basket, then Ben's. Maybe the bathroom? No laundry basket there, either, but—surprise, surprise—Jack was. Soaking in the tub, up to his armpits in steamy water, eyes closed, head back, headphones on.

She walked to the tub, past his clothes draped over a vanity chair; cell phone on top, the same one as hers. She knocked on Jack's head. His brown eyes flew open and rounded. He slid off the headphones as she asked, "What are you doing?"

"*Hell?* You never say hell."

"It's been one of those days." She peered at him as some godawful music reverberated from the headphones. "What's with the music?" She shook her head. "Never mind. I don't want to know after all."

She sat on the edge of the tub, not caring about the silk skirt or anything but being with Jack. Knowing she wasn't the only one off her trolley was comforting, in a strange sort of way. She waved a hand over the scene. "If you're listening to *that* music you've clearly lost your mind." She patted his shoulder. "I think it's an age thing."

He arched his brow. "Really?"

"You never do headphones and that's not Springsteen. You never *ever* soak in a tub, because you hate getting pruney." She picked up his hand from the water, the droplets falling onto the blue silk, making rings that would be the devil to get out. She massaged his fingers, warm and slippery. She held his hand longer than she intended. Finally, she managed to say, "See, you're getting pruney already."

"Nice skirt. And you've lost your shoes." The brown in his eyes got a shade darker. "You know how I like you barefoot. The age thing must only debilitate above the waist." He gave her a cocky smile. "Because not all of me is pruney."

Wanton hunger flickered in his eyes. "Good grief, Jack. We just had a big fight. Huge. You can't want to…"

He winked. "Lust has no memory."

"I'm forty. You're forty-one. We just did *this* yesterday. Doesn't that count for something?"

"Lust can't count, either."

She jumped up, her bare feet slipping on the damp tile as he clicked off the headphones. This was not part of her apology plan. How could she apologize when he suggested sex? Then again, sex was a much better alternative.

No way. Not again. Jack was leaving, she was staying and she was not getting involved with him and his alternatives.

"I was listening to Ben's music, trying to like it." He shook his head. "It's not going to happen. It's awful. I should buy him a copy of *Born in the U.S.A.* Now, there's real music. And I'm in the tub because Henry said it would ease sore muscles and I told Roy I'd help him in the office this afternoon. I wasn't excited about sitting in a hard wooden chair."

He held up his hand to stop her before she offered a protest to him doing the sheriff thing. "Just paperwork. That's all, I swear. And you're here because…?"

He was so sexy and wet and delicious in the tub that she wanted nothing more than to forget the apology and join him for the rest of the afternoon.

"What are you thinking?"

"Nothing." She'd answered too fast. He gave her a look that said she was lying and he knew it. Of course he didn't know for sure. Did he? "I came to apologize."

She ran her hand through her hair, then fiddled with it in the mirror because looking at Jack in the water was more temptation than she could deal with right now. "Actually, I'm here in search of the laundry basket so I could do laundry, but I couldn't find the basket and then—"

"I did it."

She cut her eyes back to him. "*You* finished my laundry? Why?"

"It's everyone's, and you have enough going on in your life right now. I threw together some spaghetti sauce. Salad's in the fridge. I told Ben he needed to help, too. He's going to make dinner tomorrow. Something about a mac-and-cheese surprise. I wonder what the surprise is."

"That he's aware of the location of the stove?" She bit back a chuckle, enjoying for a moment the connection they'd once had, before everything had gotten so complicated. "About that apology…"

She paced, keeping her back to him, which was really hard in such a little space. But how else could she think what to say with a naked, lusty, Jack Dawson—even one blurred in steamy water—five feet away? She had to apologize quickly and get out of there. "I'm sorry about the rustlers and what I said to you. You were right—about everything. We shouldn't have confronted them—we weren't sure if they had guns or not. It was a dumb idea, fueled by emotion and no brains. Not one speck of brains."

Her pacing slowed. "It could have been ugly. Very…very…ugly. Thank God you were there and not BJ and Dixie, because then I would have…there could have been…" Her stomach tightened. "A catastrophe."

BJ's and Dixie's faces—smiling, laughing—flashed through Maggie's mind, and a lump the size of Montana lodged in her chest. She stopped in her tracks. She couldn't talk. She couldn't breathe. Tears burned her eyes over what could have been because she was *so damn stupid and proud and intent on things being her way.*

"Hey, everything's okay." Jack was beside her, his hands on her shoulders. "No one got hurt. We'll get Andy back and the cattle and—"

"I don't care about the cattle." She pulled in a ragged breath. "I mean I *do* care, but not like I care about family and friends and…" Her face met his. "And you. Thank you for…being a cop."

Drops of water slid down his hard body; beads of moisture dotted his upper lip; steam spiked his eyelashes. Raw emotion burned deep in his eyes, something she'd seen only a few times before—when they married, when Ben was born, when she'd walked out of their apartment for the last time.

He held her a bit tighter. His voice was uneven as he said, "That's one I never thought I'd hear you say."

"Maybe because I've always been safe at home…till last night." She framed his face with her fingers and peered into his eyes, eyes that had seen so much violence and hate and fear. "You've lived through incredible danger that must have made the rustlers seem like nothing. How do you confront something like that day after day?"

She stood on tiptoe and kissed him, her lips caressing his once, twice, then she lost herself in the sheer joy of being near Jack and kissing him as much as she wanted to. Her fingers traced a thin scar on his jaw, then one on his left shoulder. She laid her hand over his heart, feeling his blood pump sure and strong beneath her damp palm as she considered how many times she could have lost him.

"Don't think about that," he said as if reading her mind. "We're here together now and that's all that matters."

A moan escaped her lips as she kissed him again. He slipped his arms around her and lifted her, bringing her tight to his wet, naked torso, his dampness penetrating her clothes, her bare toes no longer touching the tile.

He deepened the kiss, their mouths and breaths as one, and she folded her arms around his back, holding him tight. Her tongue matched his stroke for stroke. Her fingertips pressed into his moist flesh; his erection throbbed against her abdomen. Her heart pounded and her desire for him made her nearly delirious.

He backed her to the bathroom wall, the cool tile chilling her through the thin sodden material of her blouse. "How should we do this?" he asked. "Your room? Mine?"

"Here." She grabbed onto the shelf that held dusting powder and guest soaps, balancing herself as she wrapped her legs around his bare waist, her skirt bunching above her thighs. Hunger blazed in his eyes.

"You are so fine, so sexy." He pushed aside her silk panties and caressed her most sensitive flesh, teasing her, pleasing her as only Jack could do. She gasped as the first spirals of climax coursed through her. *"Oh, Jack."*

"I love you, babe."

And then he was inside her, filling her. Her hips arched against him, matching him thrust for thrust, making him so much a part of her. The pleasure of their lovemaking consumed every inch of her body, her mind, her soul, and she climaxed again in an inferno of pure pleasure and intimate love.

She kept her eyes closed as she rested her forehead against Jack's, savoring the feel of her legs at his bare waist, the air saturated with the aroma of hot sex.

His breaths were shallow and rapid. "I didn't plan on anything like this happening. Not that I'm sorry it did or…"

His whole body tensed. She opened her eyes and found his deep brown ones staring back at her. He sucked in a breath through clenched teeth. "Oh, Maggie."

She smiled and nipped his lower lip. "I thought so, too."

He raked a hand through his hair. *"Plan.* I didn't plan."

"I believe you."

He let her down with a suddenness she didn't expect. "That's not what I mean. What I do mean is…you could be pregnant." He paced to the tub.

She considered him for a long moment, taking in his words along with his firm back and great butt and incredible strength. "Okay."

He spun around to face her. "What do you mean, 'okay.' I can't believe—"

She went to him and placed her fingers across his lips, silencing him as a smile fell across her own lips. "Of all the things going crazy in my life right now, Jack, the one thing I could handle is a baby. Our baby."

"That's nuts. You're the busiest person I've ever met. And you're forty, for Pete's sake."

"Well, you don't have to say it like it's an affliction. And since you made the sauce and did the laundry, my brain isn't as far gone as I feared, so I'm okay there. BJ and Dixie will be there for me—they always are. A baby is a blessing."

He stepped back. "You're not thinking any clearer now than when we were out on that prairie."

"Excuse me?"

"How can you run the ranch *and* have a baby?"

She gave him a long, even look. "I'll run the ranch *and* have a baby. Women do these things all the time."

He raked his hand through his hair again. "No, that's not going to work."

"Oh, really."

"Your dad, the ranch, the new herd… You'll just have

to sell the ranch and move into town. That's the answer. It will solve all your problems. You'll be through with this buffalo nonsense and—"

"Nonsense?"

"And not have to worry about cattle being stolen, and getting hurt and whatever else—"

"Hold on, Detective." She put her finger back over his lips and this time kept it there. "If I'm pregnant I'll deal with it when the time comes and *I will not sell the ranch.* This is my home. This is my baby's home if there is a baby."

He pulled her fingers from his lips. "You're stressed out. And now you want to throw a baby into the mix? It's out of the question. You can't—"

"I can and I will and I'm not throwing anyone anywhere. You can return in another eighteen years to see your offspring graduate, or return any time you want. You can even sleep in the same room you're sleeping in now, because this ranch will be still be here, with me running it."

She snagged a towel from the rack and resisted the urge to snap it against his bare hind end to zing some sense into his brain, since his head was clearly located in that part of his anatomy at the moment.

Instead, she tossed the towel at him and watched it land on his head—nowhere near as satisfying as her first option. "Sometimes your ideas are just all wet, Jack Dawson, and—"

"Hello," said a female voice from downstairs. "Anybody home?" said a deep male voice. The female voice added, "I have pie from the Purple Sage. Yoo-hoo, Jack. Are you here? Maggie?"

Maggie's eyes rounded to match Jack's. "Dang, your parents. We have to get out of here. If they see us together they'll start making wedding plans. I have to change."

"Do you know this for sure?"

"Well, they're not burglars, Jack. They wouldn't call yoo-hoo."

"Not that," Jack whispered. "How long before we know if you're pregnant or not?"

"It's not your problem. In fact, it's not a problem at all. It's just fine." She stood tall and squared her shoulders.

"Don't hand me that crap, Maggie. I'm the father. The child is my responsibility."

"A testosterone surge in my guest bathroom does not constitute a father, in my book. Especially when that man clearly does not want another child in his life."

"I didn't say that."

"Close enough." She grabbed a canister of dusting powder from the shelf and dumped it on his head, a white cloud billowing around them. "I hereby absolve you of any and all parental responsibility. That will have to do till I get legal papers drawn up. Now you can go into town to help Roy, though you do smell like a big sissy. But you won't have to worry about a thing and you will not tell me or *my* baby how the hell to run our lives and where to live."

She stepped into the hall and resisted the overwhelming urge to slam the door behind her.

Chapter Eight

Three days later Maggie pulled the truck to a screeching stop in front of the sheriff's office. She stomped inside, stared at Roy sitting all nice and content behind his big cluttered desk and punched him in the arm.

His eyes shot wide-open. "What the hell was that for?"

"Lock me up. Do it. I'm guilty of assaulting an officer of the law. Going to jail's got to be better than going back to the ranch." She held out her hands in put-the-cuffs-on-me fashion.

Roy sat back in his chair. "Have you been tipping Dixie's flask? It's only eight in the morning. Why does your left eye keep twitching? Is that a rash on your neck?"

"It's the in-laws. They've decided to help me out because I'm so busy. I love them dearly, but…" Maggie plopped down into the chair across from Roy and leaned back, scratching her neck. She put her finger by her eye to keep it from twitching. "I don't remember them being quite this…*overwhelming* thirteen years ago. But I was younger then, more resilient, and they weren't *Trading Spaces* groupies."

"Trading what?"

"*Trading Spaces,* a TV show where people fix up each other's houses." A whimper crawled up Maggie's throat and she swallowed it. Forty-year-old women did *not* whimper. "Yesterday, Gert canceled the caterer for Ben's graduation party. She's cooking everything herself. She's taken over my kitchen and rearranged my pantry alphabetically. Last night she made new drapes for the family room…with matching pillows."

"Hey, new drapes and pillows could be nice."

"*They're chartreuse!* Jack's dad was a Chicago cop, too. I've listened to enough cop stories to keep *NYPD Blue* in scripts for a century. *Now* will you lock me up?"

Roy reached into the bottom drawer of his desk and pulled out a bottle of brandy. He set it on top. "These are desperate times. I think you need it."

She eyed the bottle and frowned. "Tempting, but probably not a good idea now, considering that…"

Her eyes met his and a silence fell between them. "You know," Roy finally said as he slid the bottle back in the desk, "when some ex-husbands and -wives see each other after a long separation, they're content to just shake hands."

"Or at least shake hands with gloves on."

He chuckled. "Now, what's really on your mind? I know you didn't land on my doorstep to yammer about your in-laws. If you're here about Andy and the cattle, there's nothing new. In spite of the bulletins, we still don't have a lead on the truck Jack saw. But if the rustlers were trying to move the cattle and Andy, they probably haven't because everyone's searching for them. Hauling a buffalo is not an everyday occurrence."

Roy stroked his jaw. "Dan Pruitt came in yesterday and said he saw some suspicious stuff going on over at Butch's place, but he didn't give me anything specific. Pruitt's one of your biggest supporters of the new herd and he's never gotten along with Butch, so I'm not certain if what he's saying's on the level or stirring up trouble."

"Right now there's another little problem I'm dealing with." She leaned forward and folded her hands on Roy's desk. "You wouldn't happen to have any information about this new girl Ben's running with, would you? He's not the same boy since he met up with her, Roy, and I'm afraid he'll do something completely stupid."

"Ah, the truth comes out." Roy leaned back in his chair. "Well, let's see. The father's had run-ins with the law. The mother's had run-ins with the law, Angel's dropped out of school and has had run-ins with the law. They've started a family tradition and it isn't a good one."

Maggie pinched the bridge of her nose and a migraine threatened. "Ben couldn't pick up with Sara Bennett or Jenna McCloud or any of the other ranchers' daughters. Oh, no, nothing so normal and easy as that. He has to run after the local junior felon. What if he suddenly decided it's cool to not finish school and forget college? What if he starts robbing banks or—"

"Doesn't sound like Ben." Roy nodded to the front window. "There's Angel right now."

Maggie jerked around in her chair and caught sight of a girl in a leopard-print short skirt, tank top with a sweater tied around her middle, wild blond hair and popping her gum. Maggie felt her eyes roll around in her head. "I have to be the worst mother on the planet."

"This has nothing to do with you."

She poked her chest with her index finger. "Are you kidding? I'm the mom. It always has to do with the mom. What's that *older woman* doing with my son?"

Maggie put her hands over her face and moaned. "What a dumb question and I don't think I want to know the answer to what she's doing with him."

"Angel hasn't gotten in trouble for a while now. She's washing dishes over at the Purple Sage. Heard she painted a mural on the back kitchen wall that's petty good. 'Course, I haven't seen it but—"

"Maybe I should have coffee—make that orange juice—over at the Sage before you lock me up."

"Are you going over there to tell Angel to stay away from Ben?"

"He's ruining his life, Roy. What in the world is he thinking? That's the trouble. He's *not!*" She threw her hands in the air. "Well, he probably is, but he's using the wrong head. I swear, the harder the male *qualities* the softer their brains. Maybe I can get her to leave him alone somehow."

"And maybe Jack can help. He was in here early this morning, holding down the fort while I ran some calls. He asked me the same questions you just did. You two need to talk more." He chuckled. "Another way of communicating."

She ignored him and said, "Jack and I promised to

butt out of Ben's business for a week, but this is turning into the longest week in recorded history, and Ben's acting so...different."

"He's growing up, Maggie. He's a man."

"He's eighteen and driving us insane." Maggie stood. "Angel, huh? That's really her name? Why do I have the feeling this girl's anything but an angel?"

JACK TOOK IN the aroma of fried eggs, bacon, sausage and fresh-baked pastries as he sat at a table by the kitchen, watching Dixie hustle about. He tried to figure out what to do about Angel and Ben. Dixie smiled at customers and chatted as she topped up empty coffee cups with one hand and snagged dirty dishes with the other. The Chicago Bulls could use her for a center...if she wasn't five-three.

"Dixie Carmichael, best waitress in Montana," Maggie said as she pulled up to the table, then slid into the bench across from Jack. "And best mom and wife—till Danny Shelton made a killing in the stock market, divorced Dixie for a supermodel, took their son and never looked back. If there's hell, Danny gets the penthouse."

"That's the most you've said to me in three days."

"That's because it's easier to talk about someone else's problems than ours. Besides, we've been so busy getting ready for the graduation party tonight we haven't had time to talk. Even if we did we'd probably start World War IV since we did III in my guest bathroom. What are you doing here, I thought your mother sent you out for torch lights?"

"What are *you* doing here? I thought you were supposed to get extra tables. And—" Jack ventured a half smile "—it wasn't *all* war."

She reddened, and this time he smiled to himself. She might be tough on the outside, but there was an *inside* Maggie, the blushing, vulnerable Maggie, the woman not quite sure of herself, who always captured his heart, just as she did now.

Her hair curled neatly around her lovely face and she wore a green blouse with a white scarf at the neck. Were those dark circles rimming her eyes? No doubt, resulting from graduation-party plans mixed with in-law burnout. "You're beat. You should sleep more."

She smirked. "*We* should sleep more." The smirk disappeared, and for a moment, neither breathed. The diner seemed devoid of anyone but the two of them. He thought of sleeping with Maggie; he'd thought about it a lot over the years, naked, all wrapped around each other, not able to get enough of each other. Making love till exhausted, then making love again. And from the spark in Maggie's eyes she remembered the very same things.

"Howdy, handsome," Dixie said, snapping him back to the moment. "Am I interrupting something, I hope?"

"No," they answered together, and much too fast to be believed.

Dixie checked Jack's coffee and refilled his cup. She eyed Maggie. "Tea or coffee?"

"Orange juice," she said with conviction, and folded her arms across her chest and stared at Jack.

He groused, "You got this all wrong. I don't mind if you're having…*orange juice*. Not at all. Orange juice is fine—I like it a lot—but not on the ranch. It makes a lot more sense to have orange juice in town and you know it."

"Ha! It's none of your business where I have orange juice."

"Yes, it is my business, dammit." Suddenly, he could see Maggie all round and voluptuous with their child. He pictured himself holding her, making love to her, watching the baby grow inside her. Which would never happen because he'd be in Chicago and she'd be raising another child alone.

Hellfire! He should be taken out and hung. How could this happen? Why was she still so irresistible to him? And why hadn't he grabbed a damn condom? He was an absolute idiot.

Dixie scrunched her nose. "What's wrong with you two? It's orange juice. Get over…"

She glanced from one to the other. "Oh. *Orange juice*. Not coffee or tea. Hmm." She looked back and forth again. "You know, orange juice is good. Not that it's any of my beeswax, but you sure enjoyed the last time you had orange juice together."

Jack glared at Dixie, giving her a silent message.

"O-kay!" She held up her hand in surrender. "Time for Dixie to change the subject, right. So, why are you two here instead of hunting for the rustlers or getting Sky Notch ready for the big do tonight?"

Jack forced a grin, glad to get off the OJ topic. "The

whole senior class is coming. No joyriding or having keggers. We have a DJ, arcade games, go-cart races, fireworks. Everyone has fun. Everyone stays out of trouble."

"Staying out of trouble—now, there's an interesting topic." Maggie hitched her chin at the double swinging doors that led to the kitchen and said to Dixie, "I hear you have a new dishwasher these days."

Dixie raised her brow. "*Aha.* Now we get to why you're here. I thought the interfering parents were back at the ranch. Yes, we have a new dishwasher, who just happens to be close to your son."

Jack looked at Dixie. "Define close."

Dixie tapped her pencil against her order pad. "Angel works hard and keeps to herself, and that's all I know about her."

"You're lying." Maggie huffed.

"I'm butting out." Dixie grinned. "And this time I mean it."

A fiftyish woman with honey-colored hair, a warm smile and a touch of sadness in her hazel eyes approached the table before Dixie left. "Maggie Moran? I'm Irene. Your father's…friend, and square-dance partner for the past several weeks."

She handed Maggie an envelope. "Would you mind giving this to Henry? I thought it might be easier on him if you delivered the letter than if it just came in the mail."

Maggie smiled, then frowned in confusion. "You can't give it to him yourself?"

Irene pressed her lips together and the sadness deepened. "I can't do that because…because I won't be seeing Henry anymore."

Jack drank his coffee. Did anything—*anything at all*—run smoothly in Whistlers Bend? Cattle? Being sheriff? Ex-wives? And now Irene with a Dear Henry letter? Irene turned to go and Maggie mouthed to him, *Do something.*

Like what, he mouthed back. Hell, he couldn't handle his own relationship and he was taking on Henry's? Oh, boy, *this* should be a huge success. He cleared his throat. "Would you join us for a cup of coffee?"

Irene glanced back. "I really should be going. I have errands and—"

"Just one cup," Jack insisted. "Since Maggie's passing on your letter to Henry?" Guilt, the ultimate motivator.

Maggie scooted over and patted the seat beside her. Irene sat on the edge as if not wanting to be there but not knowing how to get out of it. Maggie said, "Henry can be a big tease sometimes, and if he's done something to upset you he probably doesn't even realize it. Maybe if you just talk to him."

Dixie brought Maggie's juice and poured Irene coffee as she let out a sigh that seemed to come from deep inside. "It's nothing like that, dear. Henry's a wonderful man, truly." She reddened, and fiddled with a napkin. "But then, I don't have to tell you that. It's my children I'm having problems with. They don't believe Henry's *right* for me. He's ten years older and has a heart condition and…"

Irene frowned and puffed out a breath. "Oh, who the

heck am I kidding. The real reason they don't want me with Henry is that he's not their father. My George was a terrific husband and father and the kids have decided I should be content with those memories."

Dixie parked her free hand on her hip and held her coffee carafe with an air of authority. She peered down her nose at Irene. "How old are these kids?"

"In their late twenties." Irene gave Maggie a who-the-heck-is-this look as Dixie pushed into the booth beside Jack, forcing him to scoot over.

She set down the pot. "When you're twenty-something, fifty-something seems like one step from the funeral parlor. Your kids don't realize you have a lot of living to do." Dixie eyed Irene. "You *do* have a lot of living to do, right?"

"I…I guess so."

"Well, good, 'cause Henry sure does. He's a live-wire, that one." She chuckled, then continued. "But memories don't keep a body warm on a cold Montana night, if you get my meaning."

Irene nibbled her bottom lip. "You're right about that. It does get…*cold* here. Very cold come winter." She blushed again and raced on. "I know I'll miss Henry a great deal, but I don't want to cause a riff in the family. We have a wonderful family, you see."

Dixie tsked, "As long as you do what your kids want, you have a wonderful family." She leaned her elbow on the table. "Seems to me you have two choices here. Somebody's going to be unhappy. Should it be you without Henry, *or* your kids because you're *with* Henry? They're young. They'll get over it. Will you?"

Dixie nodded and stood, snatching up her pot. "And if I were you and I did the choosing, I sure as blazes wouldn't choose to be unhappy for all the years to come. What kind of sense does that make? None—that's what kind." She winked. "No charge for that little bit of café psychology." She turned in a flourish and left.

Maggie patted Irene's hand. "What Dixie's trying to say is—"

"I have rocks for brains?"

"Or," Maggie said, "that your kids are running your life. And that's okay...*if* it's okay with you. But if it isn't, eventually you'll resent them, and that's not a happy family. No one likes to be controlled, Irene. Not me—" she eyed Jack "—and not you."

"And not Ben?" Jack said as his gaze met Maggie's.

Irene opened her purse and removed her wallet. She selected larger bills from the back and put them on the table, then swept the letter from Maggie's fingers. She ripped it into small pieces; the remains fluttered to the table like confetti. "Coffee and juice are on me and the tip is for your friend. Deep in my heart I suspected all those things. I just needed to hear them out loud to get my gumption up to do what I nccd to do."

"You know," Jack said with a smile, "if you encourage Dixie like this, there may be no stopping her. She'll probably set up a booth with The Buttinski Is In written on it."

Irene laughed as she left. "I don't imagine we could stop her if we wanted to."

Dixie moseyed over and nodded at the retreating

woman. "What do you suspect happens now? I hate to see Henry hurt."

Maggie held up the bills in one had and the confetti in the other. "Irene wouldn't have left you this tidy sum and this debris if she hadn't agreed with you."

"Well I'll be." Dixie beamed as she stuffed the bills into her apron, then scooped the shredded letter into her palm. "I do believe I hear another cute little Stetson calling my name. *Oh, Dixie girl, come buy me. I'm just waiting for you.* Black sounds good to me, with a gold band. I should have started handing out advice long ago."

"You did. You were six and told Sally McGuire to punch Steve Riley in the nose for stealing her lunch money. Now you just got paid for it. Tell me, was that little lecture about not interfering aimed at Irene…or us and a certain dishwasher?"

Dixie twitched her hips. "Remember ages ago, when you were eighteen and full of yourself and thought you had all the answers? Did you listen to anything—even one darn thing—your parents said?"

Jack rubbed the back of his neck. "Oh, crap."

"Exactly. I went through this last year when my Sean graduated. Gave him so much advice he didn't speak to me for a month and only came to visit for a week instead of the whole summer, afraid I'd give him even more unwanted advice. He wrote *Dear Abby* about his interfering mother and signed his real name. How embarrassing was that. I was so afraid he'd make the wrong decisions about where to go to college, what courses to sign up for, what dorm to live in, what clothes to pack. You name it—I had an opinion."

Maggie sighed. "Why don't kids come into the world with instructions tattooed on their little heels?"

"Forget instructions. I want a guarantee that says, *This product will perform, and you won't have a care in the world or you will be refunded all your work and worry and you get a villa in Tuscany.*"

Dixie grinned and spread her arms over Jack and Maggie. "We all deserve the villa...but the kids still need to make up their own minds."

Dixie winked and left as Maggie turned to Jack. "I better call your mother and tell her we're on our way." She picked out her gray cell phone and frowned. "I forgot to recharge. I always forget to recharge."

Jack reached into his pocket and got his. "Use mine." He studied the phones. "They're almost the same." He gave her a smug grin. "Bet I got a better deal."

She gave him a sassy smile. "In your dreams. I'll tell your mom we had to get some business straightened out."

Maggie made the call and Jack got the drift from Maggie's side of the conversation, which consisted of yes and yes and more yesses, that his mother wanted action now. Maggie disconnected, gritted her teeth, dropped the phone into her purse and stood. "We gotta go right this minute or your mother'll string us both up. She needs those tables and lights at the ranch within the hour. Ben's graduation *must* be perfect."

Jack snatched his phone from the table and exhaled.

"As much as I love that woman I hate when she does perfect. She'll drive us all nuts by tonight."

He took Maggie's hand, amazed how a little zing always zipped through him when he touched her or simply glanced her way. He'd never adjust to being without her.

"GRADUATION STARTS in an hour and a half," Maggie said to Jack and Ben as she sat on the end of Ben's bed and concentrated on their reflections in the mirror over Ben's dresser. She didn't have to be here, of course. The men could tie ties without her supervision, but the three of them together like this was rare.

There should have been more of these times, though staying in Chicago with kamikaze Jack was more than her blood pressure would have allowed, though being apart hadn't been a picnic, either.

Jack held up the narrow end of the tie and said, "Just wrap the wide side around the skinny side like this."

Same dark slightly wavy hair, same set to their stubborn jaw, same stance, same build, same smile, same eyes. Like father like son never rang so true.

Ben flipped the tie around, imitating Jack. "Why do we have to wear ties to graduation? We're going to have on those dorky long robes. No one will see—"

"The robes don't come all the way to your neck," Jack said. "You'll see the tie. Think of this as the last bit of torture high school puts you through."

The guys chuckled; Maggie felt her throat tighten. *Last.* The word fell over her like a bucket of cold water.

"You've got that worried look, Mom. What's wrong?" Ben's eyes met hers in the mirror.

"You know, it's those PTA meetings. Whatever will I do the second Tuesday night of each month?" She held out her hands in fake concern. "How *will* I ever fill the time?"

"You don't want me to leave, do you?"

"Are you kidding. I'm turning your bedroom into a sewing room. Isn't that what moms do when their kids go off to college?"

"You don't sew and I *am* coming back. It's not like I'm leaving forever."

"Of course not." She wanted to make some snappy comeback but couldn't because the thought of Ben not in this room every night was eating her up. He *was* leaving, and that was good, she encouraged herself. It meant he was still going to college and hadn't backed out. But…how had eighteen years passed so quickly? A blink of an eye and Ben was all grown up.

She forced a bright smile. "University of Denver is only a plane flight away."

Jack shrugged into his suit coat. "I'll get the camera—don't want to forget it." He left and Maggie stood and turned Ben toward her. "Here, let me finish that." She flipped his tie into a neat knot the way she had for so many Christmases, Easters, dances and special dates. She patted the knot at his neck. "Now you're perfect."

He smiled down at her, his eyes twinkling. "You always say that."

Her heart swelled with pride and ached with the

promise of losing him to college, life in general and especially *that girl*. Maggie nearly gasped. *Good grief! Was that the problem with Angel…at least part of it?* For the first time, Ben had another woman in his life?

She kissed him on the cheek and prayed she wasn't so narrow-minded. "Happy graduation, Ben. I love you and want only the best things for you. Now I'll see if your grandparents are ready. We don't want to be late. I tried to talk them out of the limo they hired in Rocky Fork to take us to the high school gym. Pray I succeeded."

She started for the door and Ben took her arm. "Mom, wait. I want to talk to you for a minute."

Oh, God, Angel's pregnant was all Maggie could think of. *He's going to marry her and they're going to live in a commune in Arizona and raise goats.*

Ben kissed her on the cheek. "Thanks for everything. You've always been there for me, carted me to practices, Boys Scouts, baseball, basketball, football games. Taught me to ride and love the ranch. You taught me almost everything."

He reached into his pocket and pulled out a little gold medal with a tiger on the front. "The baseball team voted me Eager Cat, the guy everyone goes to to get the job done." He put the medal in Maggie's hand. "For me, that's been you. You've always been my Eager Cat, always in my corner. You're the best, Mom. Thanks." Then he kissed her again and walked out the door.

Maggie plopped down on the edge of the bed and stared at the medal in her palm. She looked to the door. Ben was a man in every sense. Loyal and kind and considerate and thoughtful and honest. *Ben was his father.* She could not ask for anything more than that. And she had to trust in that.

"Hey," Jack said from the doorway. "Are you okay?"

She smiled and nodded. "Terrific, actually. I don't think life gets much better than this."

"Well, you might want to hold real tight to that. Angel's downstairs. Ben invited her to his graduation. Irene's here. Her daughter threw her out of the house when she said she wasn't giving up Henry. Her bags are in her car and I told her she could stay in the room I'm using and I'll bunk on the couch. My parents got the limo. It's one of those stretch babies and it's parked out front."

Maggie and Jack laughed, the moment filling her with more joy than she thought possible. She finally managed to say, "I believed things got easier when you got older. That we'd have all the answers. Where's this infused wisdom, rite of passage, settled lifestyle of the middle-aged woman?"

She spread her arms wide. "Since I turned forty, I feel like I got shot out of a cannon and I don't know where I'm landing." She closed her fingers around the medal. "But for some reason I wouldn't have it any other way."

He snapped her picture.

"Why'd you do that?"

"Forty suits you, Maggie Moran. You've never been more beautiful, more competent, more caring, more charming. You're an incredible woman and I love you more now than ever. I just have no idea what the hell we're going to do about it."

Chapter Nine

The pale gray of dawn inched over the mountains as the last of the kids drove down the gravel driveway of Sky Notch on their way to the McClouds' for breakfast after the all-night party. Jack waved, then ambled toward the big white tent. *Amble* was top speed at the moment. Stakeouts, takedowns, busts had not prepared him for a night with teenagers. *Like anything could!* Where'd they get all their energy? Did everything have to be so *loud?* His head throbbed; his ears rang.

Gold and blue streamers drooped from the tent top; dilapidated mortarboard centerpieces and half-filled plastic cups cluttered the tables; white folding chairs sat helter-skelter.

Jack all but collapsed onto one of the chairs and gave a little salute to the DJ collecting his equipment on the other side of the dance floor. The guy looked as beat as Jack felt. A song played, something slow and quiet that Jack didn't recognize. Then again, that was nothing new, since he hadn't recognized one damn piece of music all night long. Wasn't *scratching* what people and animals did when they itched? How'd it get to be a DJ term associated with music?

Maggie shuffled in and plopped down across from him. She didn't say a word but leaned her head back, facing the ceiling, and closed her eyes. Her rumpled pink blouse pulled across her rounded breasts; her long white gauzy skirt flowed around her shapely legs. Desire stirred his insides…and his outsides.

Damn. He dropped a mortarboard centerpiece in his lap, the hat part hiding the obvious. Not all of him felt tired. Hell, when it came to Maggie *that* part of his anatomy never tired, at least, not for long, but he didn't have to advertise his condition to the DJ.

Maggie kicked off one pink sandal and it did a little flip into the air, then the other sandal. She wiggled her toes in the trampled grass. "Well, roughrider, we did it and we lived to tell the tale…I think."

She lifted one eye open. "Actually, it was your idea, with your parents bringing it all together. As a parent of a graduating senior I appreciate it, but my poor pooped body just won't recognize that fact right now. Why is there a centerpiece in your lap?"

"I'm admiring its artistic beauty."

She sighed. "Temporary insanity. I should have warned you that teenagers can do that to a parent."

Jack's cell phone rang and he slid it from his pocket and answered it. "It was for you. The rental company. Said they'll be here at noon to collect the tables and chairs."

"Why is a call for me on your phone?"

He looked at the phone for a long moment, trying to think. "This one must be yours. We've switched them somehow. We'll switch back later."

He slid the phone in his pocket as she closed her eyes and put her feet in Jack's lap. "I'm so tired. Let's sleep right here in the chairs. We'll tell the rental company we'll bring them back later. Wake me next week."

He massaged her left foot, then the right. Hot-pink nail polish, shapely ankles. "I'll be gone next week, Maggie."

The words caught in his throat and his chest tightened into a painful knot. *Again* he was saying goodbye to her. *Again* he hated it with every bone in his body. *Again* he had no idea what to do about it.

Her eyes opened slowly and they stared at each other. "You'll visit?"

"Yeah, I'll visit. Maybe in nine months from now I'll visit."

She gave him a sly grin. "That's one way to get you back in Whistlers Bend to massage my poor tired tootsies."

Angel poked her head into the tent. She gave a shy little wave, then came over. She shifted her weight and bit at her bottom lip. "Uh, I love your ranch. And…this was a great party. Thanks for having me, even though I'm not graduated." She smiled self-consciously, then rushed on. "But I am getting my GED in a few months. Ben talked me into it and he's helping me study."

Jack sat a little straighter, considering the statement. Study? Voluntarily? Ben? The age of miracles hadn't ended. "Where is he? Thought you'd be gone by now."

"He's in the house, changing because I spilled a Coke on his shirt. I'm kind of a klutz." She reddened. "He's a great guy. The best," Angel gushed. "I hope he finds a girl who really appreciates him."

Jack felt his eyes round. "Aren't you his girl?"

Angel shook her head, sending her long blond hair dancing around her slender shoulders. "It's not like that between us. We're friends. Good friends. And if I hadn't stolen his truck and if he hadn't come after me, I never would have met him and gone back to school and…"

Maggie sat straight up in her chair and Angel gazed from Jack to Maggie and back. "You don't know about any of this, do you? I asked him to not say anything till I got myself together, but I just thought he'd tell you two, since you're his parents."

She swallowed. "I sort of stole Ben's truck." She eyed Jack, embarrassed. "Guess you think I'm awful, you being a cop and all. Anyway, he chased after me for five blocks, and when I had to stop for the train to pass he caught up and he yelled and screamed a lot and threw a fit right there in the middle of the street and everybody was looking and then my stomach growled and he took me to get something to eat. We had pancakes."

Jack asked, "Why did you steal the truck?"

"To get out of town." She shuffled her feet. "He convinced me to stay and move out of my parents' house. Got me some furniture and he talked to Dixie and helped me get a job at the Purple Sage. It's not much, but it's better than stealing cars and I get free food. Can't beat that." She gave a nervous laugh.

"Hey," Ben said from the tent opening. He sauntered over to Angel and dropped his arm around her, grinning at his parents. "I wanted to introduce you to Angel, but she said she wasn't ready." He winked. "I'm glad she changed her mind." He rubbed her arm and smiled down at her. "See, I told you they wouldn't bite."

He kissed her hair. "If we don't get a move on, all the pancakes at the McClouds' will be gone. You know I gotta have my pancakes. I bet they have blueberry."

Angel poked him in the ribs and giggled, sounding like a little girl who hadn't had all that much to laugh about. "How can you eat so much?"

"How can you eat so little? Race you to the truck, half-pint?"

"Hey, who you calling half-pint." Angel waved to Jack and Maggie, then took off like a shot.

Ben chuckled as he watched her running like the wind, hair flying, feet barely touching the ground, a sense of happiness in every step. He nodded her way. "She loves to win. Not that she's had much practice at it. She's not really used to winning…yet. See, she's a nice girl after all, and we're not driving off to a commune to raise goats."

Maggie's mouth dropped. "How'd you know?"

"You're my mom. That's what moms do." He laughed and took off after Angel.

Jack shook his head in utter disbelief. "What the hell just happened?"

"Growing up means more than buying a larger shoe size and going to college. Our son gets that. Do you realize that some people never get what life's about? But at eighteen our son does. He listens to people and sees what they need. He knows me as well as I know him." She made a face. "That's kind of scary."

She reached over and grasped Jack's hand. "He's a wonderful man, Jack. He's…you."

Peace and love filled his heart and his soul. Not something he experienced all that often. He held Maggie's hand in his. "That's the nicest thing anyone's ever said to me."

"I'm glad you think so, because it's true, every word of it."

Another song drifted their way. "Well, I'll be. I recognize this one." He hummed a few notes, then grinned his appreciation to the DJ, who nodded as he walked out of the tent.

Jack stood and tugged Maggie up beside him. "Let's dance. The DJ's playing this one for us."

She balanced on her shoeless tiptoes and wound her arms around his neck. She snuggled, burying her face in his neck. He did the same, inhaling the scent of warm sunshine and cool mountain air in her hair. Her fingers felt like velvet touching his neck; her body next to his was heaven on earth. He held her tight, never wanting to let her go. He crooned, barely a whisper.

Their bodies swayed to the familiar "Unchained Melody" and she kissed his neck, then glanced up at him, her eyes sparkling with the fun of it all. "You've never sung to me before."

"I don't sing. More like a croak." He kissed her forehead. "There're a lot of things I should have done. I should have danced with you more, taken more time off when we were married. I should have locked us in the bedroom for days with only champagne and chocolate and silk sheets and flushed my damn pager down the toilet. I should have, *somehow,* found a way to keep us together."

He kissed her, her warm, sweet lips reminding him again what he'd given up. He ached, not just from his own physical need, but for what the two of them could have and didn't. "I want to make love to you, Maggie. Now."

"No," she said on a sigh as she closed her eyes. "In four days you're out of here, and all I'll dream about is us making love. I can't keep doing this, Jack. It's torture. God, is it torture. Having you and letting you go, having you and letting you go. You're...addictive. And when you leave, it's cold turkey for me."

She stepped away from him. Her eyes sad, her face drawn. "I can't do cold anymore. I'm forty. I've got to move on, and making love to you is not moving on."

He put his hand on her shoulder, his insides feeling as if lacerated by a knife. "What do you mean by 'moving on'?"

"I don't know." She stepped back again. "Just...on. As in not constantly dreaming of you."

"You do that?"

She waved her hand over the empty tent. "You don't see anyone else here, do you? No suitors sniffing around. No gallant male waiting in the wings with bouquets of roses." She put her hands on her hips. "I want gallant. I want roses. I want sniffing. And I can't get any of those things when you're the only man in my thoughts. No one can compete with you. I have to let you go."

She shook her head. "I need sleep. I'm not up to discussing you and me and how we don't work." She picked up her sandals, then turned for the door, muttering, "Heck, I haven't been up to that for thirteen years, but I'm going to change."

Jack watched her leave. He followed her to the entrance and leaned against the pole as she made her way across the dewy grass, her long skirt swaying at her ankles as she walked, her pink sandals dangling in her right hand. She didn't head for the house, dark with everyone asleep inside, but bypassed it and aimed for the main barn.

He wanted her and he knew she wanted him but... There was always a *but*. And what the hell was this crap about *moving on* and changing? His insides blazed. *Move on*...with whom? Change how? *"Like hell!"*

Fatigue vanished as Jack tromped off across the grass. She was his, dammit. At least while he was here. It might not be right or even rational, but it was true. Every inch of her delectable skin, every strand of her shimmering hair, every curve of her lush body—all were his.

Quiet hugged the earth. A morning breeze rippled through the pines, sending their spiky branches nodding. Clouds hovered over the mountains, promising rain in the valley. Determination pushed him to walk faster. A storm brewed in more places than the sky.

He entered the main barn, taking in the familiar

aroma of hay mixed with oats and barley and warm horse flesh. He gazed around. Butterfly whinnied and Jack stroked his nose. Okay, where the hell was Maggie? A sprig of hay fell on his shoulder. The loft.

He climbed the wood ladder across from Butterfly's stall. Maggie sat on a bale, gazing out the open loft doors.

"What are you doing up here?" she asked, without facing him.

"I've come for you."

She turned and sighed. She rested her elbow on her knee and put her chin in her palm. She waved her other hand as if shooing a fly. "Go away." She yawned. "We're done."

He strode toward her, her eyes widening with each of his steps, fatigue fading. "Seems to me you've been the one calling all the shots since I got here."

She sat up straight. "Ha! What was that little tryst in the bathroom? I didn't call the shots there."

"I got a hell of a lot of cooperation and—" he raised his left brow and smiled wickedly while advancing "—I was just getting warmed up. I didn't have to call anything. But I'm calling now. You're mine."

"No, Jack!" She jumped up. "You've got that look."

"I've got a hell of a lot more than a look." He took another step toward her.

"You're making this worse…for both of us. You have to move on, too."

"Right now I'm moving on…toward you. Where are your ranch hands?"

"Downstairs, guarding my virtue."

"They're twenty years too late."

She stepped back and tripped over the bale of hay, arms flailing, eyes huge, landing with her legs on the bale, the rest of her spread-eagled on the floor.

"Least you didn't land in a cold stream." He folded his arms and winked down at her. "And you flat on your back is pretty much what I had in mind, for starters."

"No. No, no, no!" She held up her hands and shook her head at him.

He sat on the bale and studied her. Skirt bunched at her thighs, legs exposed for his viewing, hair mussed as if he'd already done what he planned.

He unbuttoned his shirt. "Do you have any idea what things I want to do to you?"

"*Want* something else. How about coffee and a doughnut?"

His focus stayed on her. "How I want to touch you where only I know about."

She bit her bottom lip.

"Kiss behind your left ear and listen to you gasp and whimper."

She bit her knuckle.

"Put my tongue to your navel and watch how you quiver all over." He touched her cheek. "Have my fingers teasing and stroking other soft places that are hot and wet just for me…for our lovemaking and—"

"Jack."

He shrugged out of his shirt, the morning air chilling his naked torso. "I want you to feel me against you, Maggie. On you. Deep inside you." He unbuckled his belt. "I want to spread your thighs wide. Have your knees over my shoulders. Hold your firm bottom in my palms—"

"*Jack!*"

He pulled off his boots. "Taste the sweet secrets that I remember so well and miss so damn much that sometimes I can't even breathe."

He stood, pulled a little blue package from his pocket, then slid off his jeans and briefs. Her eyes rounded as she eyed him in, implying his Viagra days were some time off. "And that's just me getting started."

She licked her lips and let out a long, appreciative resigning sigh. "Oh, Jack."

He grinned. "Do I understand that to mean yes?"

She closed her eyes, slapped her palm to her forehead and flopped back onto the wood floor. "How can you do this to me? How can I be such a slut? How can I want you so badly it...hurts?"

"Babe, what I have planned is not going to hurt, and making love cannot be any more torture than not. That we both agree on. Besides, forty is a woman's sexual prime." He growled, "And I intend to get my share."

She propped herself up on her elbows again. "What are you going to do—fly in here every few months, strip buck naked, refresh yourself from my sexual prime and then leave?"

He tore open the foil pouch and covered himself, then helped her up, her skirt flowing back over her legs...temporarily. He undid the top button on her blouse. He didn't look her in the eyes because he couldn't promise her anything, not one damn thing, except for now. "You know what my job is like. It's a vacuum. People get sucked in and don't leave."

"You mean *you* don't leave." A gentle rain patted the roof as she tipped his chin so their eyes met. He'd never seen eyes so blue, so mysterious as Maggie's. He peeled her pink blouse from her shoulders, uncovering delicate, tender skin.

"Yeah," he sighed on a breath as her intimate scent washed over him. "I don't leave. But I'm here now and so are you. That's got to be one hell of a lot better than us apart, at least for the moment."

He ran his fingers down her back, as her lips parted and her breaths quickened. He unsnapped her bra and her eyes darkened as the silky material fell from her shoulders, revealing breasts lush, round, made for a man's hands…and mouth. "You're beautiful."

He held one tempting breast in each palm and a moan escaped her lips, her nipples hardening as he traced his thumb across the now-firm nubs. He watched them pink under his touch. "I love how you respond to me so quickly, so passionately. All the way."

He bent his head and kissed the tender flesh, his tongue delighting in her silky texture, in the heat of her on his lips.

Their eyes met, hers clouded with desire and longing, turning him on even more. She kissed him hungrily, saying *I want you, too.*

He released her breasts and trailed his fingers down her midriff, her muscles shuddering in his path. He hooked his thumbs into the waistband of her skirt and he slowly slipped the wispy material over her womanly hips, her fine bottom, then let the material flow to her ankles in a soft circle.

Only her panties covered her now, cream-colored lace, the last obstruction to seeing every delicious inch of his Maggie.

Just looking at Maggie made his erection throb, bringing him almost to the point of pain. He couldn't remember ever feeling so taut with the desire to have her. Maybe because this would be the last time for a long time; maybe because he cherished her now more then ever.

He ran his hands inside her panties. In a flip of his wrist, he ripped them off.

Her eyes flew open as the patch of silk fluttered to the floor. "Hey, those were new. Fifteen dollars for six inches of silk and lace. Victoria's Secret, not on sale. Why'd you do that?"

"They were in the way." His skin burned; his muscles ached. "I'll send you a check," he promised. "I want my hand on you, all of you."

"Do you always get what you want?"

"Now I do." He breathed the words more than said them.

He gripped her bottom and brought her swift and tight to him. She gasped and her breasts swelled against him.

She whimpered, then pulled back, her eyes wild. "You know—" she panted "—that sexual peak thing you were talking about?" She wiggled out of his embrace, fluffed her skirt over the hay and lay down on it, holding her arms open to him. "It's peaking really quick."

He gave her a wicked smile. "Good."

He went down beside her and cupped the cluster of silky brown curls at the apex of her legs, his big hand covering her completely. The darkness of his skin contrasted with her pale flesh. "So soft, so delicious, so secretive."

"Jack, I don't want adjectives."

"Then how about this." He slid his hand downward into the crevice of her legs and glided his fingers into the hot, wet, swollen folds he knew so well. Her eyes dilated and her mouth opened as her hips bucked in primal instinct against his hand, taking his fingers deeper. "Oh, Jack!"

Then he felt her hand close gently around his erection, sending ecstasy through his body. She stroked him, slowly at first, her touch and rhythm perfect, then faster. "You are incredible."

He kissed her hard as he eased his fingers from her—silky, slippery. He placed himself over her and slowly slid himself into the place where he most wanted to be. Her legs embraced him, her eyes widened. The scent of sex and profound intimacy filled the loft.

She met his thrust, then again and again. Her little cries of delight came faster, louder, bringing him closer to the brink, till they climaxed in a burst of mutual pleasure and all-consuming love of husband and wife that would last forever.

MAGGIE LAY STILL, feeling Jack's heavy breathing return to normal. She held him and threaded her fingers through his hair, now damp with perspiration. Then she placed a kiss at his temple. Although she missed making love with Jack, she missed the moments like this most of all.

"You are an incredible man, Jack Dawson."

He stirred, then rolled over, taking her with him. He smiled lazily up at her, his eyes loving. "What makes you say that?" He brushed her hair back from her face and tucked it behind her left ear.

"You get your way and I'm not sorry that you do."

"Hate to break it to you, but it's not just *my* way. If you hadn't wanted to make love, we wouldn't have."

She rested her forehead against his, staring deep into his eyes. "But I did, even if I'll miss you all the more later on. I cherish being close to you, Jack. Making love to you makes me feel like a special woman."

"Babe, you *are*. Strong and independent and caring and compassionate, and hell-on-wheels in the sack." He blew out a puff of air. "Wow."

"I think that's you, especially the last part." She giggled and kissed his cheek. "But this isn't the sack. We never get to the sack."

A breeze drifted in through the open doors as Jack trailed his fingers up and down her spine. "Spontaneity is good."

"What's your take on seduction?"

"Seduction's even better." His brown eyes darkened

to a color of rich chocolate. "How'd we ever wind up divorced?"

"Because bed—or any substitute for bed—has never been our problem. It's when we get out of bed that all our problems break loose."

"That means…" He brought her over, pinning her under him as she laughed. "We're not supposed to get out of bed or any substitute for it."

He balanced himself on his elbows, gazing down at her. "I'll try to get back here as often as possible, every few months—and not just to take advantage of your forty-year-old sexuality."

He tweaked her nose. "I'm not doing another thirteen years without you, Maggie, in or out of bed. I can't." His words were a declaration, a promise.

"And every time you show up you're going to harangue me into selling the ranch and moving to town?"

He shook his head. "I won't do that, I swear. But I'm going to help you out as much as I can when I do show up. Henry's got Irene on his mind now. You have the hands, but you still need help. Deal?"

She nodded. "Deal. As long as you remember whose ranch this is."

"How could I forget?"

"The hands will be coming in any minute to change horses and get supplies. They've been on rotations bunking down with the cattle till we find out who's behind this." She pushed Jack away and he flopped over into the hay. "Whoever thinks hay is soft is nuts. It sticks like needles."

He stood and slid off the condom. "Okay, what the hell do I do with *this* thing?"

She pushed herself up and dusted off. "What do you usually do with them?"

"Hey, I'm a virgin. This is my first time in a barn."

She laughed, plucked her panties from the floor and held them up. "Since they're already shot…"

"Forget my check. I'll buy you new ones." He wiggled his brows wickedly. "It'll be my greatest of pleasures to buy you many, many so I can take them off many, many times."

She watched him dress while doing the same. *Now what to do?* 180 or so pounds of delicious male virility just trampled her *we gotta move on* plans right into the dirt. Jack lived inside her, with her every minute of the day, and it would be worse now than ever.

"Let's go." He faced her. "Don't look so serious. This time it'll work between us, Maggie. I promise. As you told Ben, Denver is only a plane ride away. The same's true of Chicago."

She started for the ladder. "You have to get on the plane first, Jack. When you return, will you forget Chicago even has an airport?"

He followed her. "Going through O'Hare is an experience you can't forget no matter how hard you try." He grinned. "And now I'll have a special reason to remember it. Catching a plane back to you." He nodded out the door. "It's not raining. Race you to the house?"

She flew off in a dead run, Jack at her side, keeping pace with her.

"You're not going to let me win, are you?" She panted, vowing to get more exercise.

He stopped suddenly and caught her waist. Laughing, she fell into his arms and he lifted her up, swinging her around. Shafts of sunlight split the gray clouds, and the fresh scent of rain and grass hung in the air. For a moment, everything was perfect—perfect setting, perfect time of her life, perfect man. When this happened—and it didn't happen often—the mature, experienced part of her always wondered, *How long can it last?*

He brought her to the porch, where Maggie opened the front door, and carried her over the threshold, saying, "It's like getting married all over again."

The words hung between them like a challenge, or was it more like a possibility? But how could it work?

Henry's voice rang out from the kitchen. "Whoever's at the front door, come on in and make yourself at home. Fresh coffee's on the stove."

Jack set her down and kissed her. He stroked her cheek, then kissed her once more. "We'll talk later."

"But how can we—"

"Just think about it, okay. Think about *us*. It's our turn, Maggie."

And she did think about it, all the way down the hall and into the kitchen. How could she and Jack make something work that had failed so miserably before? Who would give up what? How could *that* make anyone happy?

When they reached the kitchen, Irene sat at the table and Henry across from her. Maggie grabbed the pot from the stove and topped off Henry's cup. "You two are up early, considering no one around here got any sleep last night. I suppose Gert and Edward are sacking in."

She nodded at Irene and Henry. "Thanks for helping with the party and the kids and serving food and everything else. I don't know what I would have done without you all."

"It was our pleasure." Henry grasped Irene's hand. "And, we never made it to bed. I have news. Great news. I've asked Irene to marry me and she's accepted."

Irene blushed. "I took that talk at the diner with both of you and Dixie real serious." She looked at Henry with adoring eyes. "I'm so glad I did."

Maggie set the pot back on the stove. "That's wonderful. I'm thrilled for both of you. You deserve all the happiness in the world. We need champagne."

She went to her father and kissed him on the cheek, then did the same to Irene. Jack bear hugged Henry as Maggie headed for the fridge. She hadn't seen Henry this radiant in years. Irene was the perfect mate for him. "This calls for a toast."

Maggie opened the fridge door, looking for the extra champagne she'd bought when she, Dixie and BJ had gone on the great rustler hunt. "We should put an addition on the house, maybe a new wing on the west side so you'll get the sunset. Or maybe we can build you a new place. The north pasture is lovely and easily accessible from the back road."

"No need," Henry offered. "I got it all figured out. I'm selling the ranch."

Chapter Ten

Maggie felt her stomach lurch. Her throat tightened as she faced Henry. Had he really said what she thought he'd said? *Nah, impossible.* Sky Notch was his life as much as it was hers. His grandfather had built the place, brought in herds, raised his family here and taught Henry the business, just as Henry had taught her.

Maggie grabbed the counter for support and pulled in a steadying breath. "You're not really selling Sky Notch. Why would you want to do that? You're just selling part of it for a new road, right?"

Henry smiled and dusted his hands as if ridding himself of all his problems. "Nope, the whole shebang. It's the perfect answer to everything. Irene and I will live in town. Much easier life there. All this rigmarole over Andy and trying to start a new herd and working sunup to sundown to keep the place from getting bought up is just putting off the inevitable. It's tough work, Maggie, just like Jack said."

Henry winked at Jack, then continued, "What kind of life is that for a town girl and what kind of life is that when you're my age?"

Jack was in on this?

"Part of this ranch is yours and you'll get a share of the proceeds. The conglomerates are offering a good price now. If we wait, we could lose out. You can go back to your graphic design work." He kissed Irene and smiled. "Everything's perfect."

"What do you mean *like Jack said?*"

Henry beamed. "It was his suggestion and it makes prefect sense for me and Irene. And then there's you and Jack. The two of you are getting along." Henry grinned. "I can tell. This will give you an opportunity to see if you can work things out and get back together like you should be. Sky Notch will just get in the way of that. Irene and I will be happy in town. Jack might be happy in Whistlers Bend, or you go back to Chicago. Without the ranch in the way you can figure it out."

She felt dizzy and queasy. "It's not that simple, Dad."

"Sure it is. Where's the problem? The only thorn in our side is Sky Notch. Ben is going to school and into business. There's no one to leave the ranch to. Why not sell now, when we can enjoy ourselves and our family?" He gave her a bright-eyed look. "Right?"

No, it wasn't right at all. Maybe this was some bad dream and she'd wake up. But the expression on Henry's face suggested definite reality.

How could this happen? How could he think she wanted to sell the ranch? Yes, it was a lot of work, but it was home, the one constant in her life. She wanted to yell and scream and throw things, but ruining Henry and Irene's day was not the answer. There had to be an answer...somewhere.

Implosion threatened. Therapy. She needed therapy immediately. She flipped the oven to four-fifty and pulled out her rolling pin. Images of whacking Jack over the head flashed through her brain. But she couldn't do that to an original Martha Stewart rolling pin. However, the cast-iron skillet sitting on the stove looked pretty indestructible. If Jack hadn't put this idea in her father's head he never would have come up with it on his own.

She grabbed a bowl from the shelf and threw in handfuls of flour, then added baking powder. Henry's eyes opened wide. "Oh, my. You're baking. Are you okay? Is this upsetting you? I really believe it's the best answer for all of us."

"I'm not upset, Dad. The ranch is a lot of hard work." She smiled hugely, hoping she didn't overdo the toothy part. She added salt. "Big fluffy biscuits would taste good, don't you think? It's breakfast time. Gert and Edward will be up soon."

She pitched in a stick of butter, sending a cloud of flour into the air, then added three pinches of sugar. "Everyone's hungry. That's all. Nothing else." She cut in the shortening with more enthusiasm than normal, picturing Jack's sorry interfering hide with every slice.

"I don't know if we're *that* hungry," Henry commented as he watched. "Did you just crack the bowl?"

She whipped in milk with her wooden spoon, thinking of using it on Jack, pounding him about the neck and shoulders. "If living in town makes you and Irene happy, that makes me happy, too. You're entitled to live wherever you want."

And, she wanted to add as she turned the dough onto the pastry board, *so am I.* But she didn't say so. If Henry thought selling the ranch upset her as much as it did he'd never do it, and that wasn't fair to him, either. *But what to do?*

She attacked the dough with her rolling pin. *Take that, Jack Dawson, and that, for not keeping your big mouth shut.* "This engagement is such great news I'm going to run into town and tell Dixie and BJ later on."

Henry held up the phone. "Maybe you should call. You haven't had any sleep. You have to be dead tired...*or something.* Uh, Maggie, I think you dented the countertop."

She stamped out circles with a solid *whap, whap, whap,* ignoring her father, and tossed the biscuits onto the baking sheet. "I'll go into town tonight. This is the kind of news I want to tell in person. Fact is, we should have an engagement party. Introduce Irene to all our friends."

Have a tombstone made for Sky Notch.

She slid the biscuits into the oven and smiled, not showing as much teeth this time. No need to scare her future stepmother. "They'll be done in seventeen minutes. There's blueberry jam in the fridge."

She dumped the dirty utensils into the sink, kissed her father, patted Irene's hand, leaving it slightly covered with flour, then headed for the stairs. Fake enthusiasm lasted only so long, and even baking didn't relieve the stress, though elbowing Jack in the ribs as she passed by him helped.

He grunted, then followed her up the stairs. "It wasn't like you think," he whispered as he rubbed his side and passed the room where his parents slept.

"Oh, really." She spun around and glared as she entered her room, leaving Jack framed in the doorway. "What part of *Jack's idea* didn't I hear correctly?" she muttered.

"Henry was having trouble with Irene and I suggested a compromise to get her back. She chose Henry over her own family and he'd like to please her by moving into town."

"Which happened to involve selling my home!"

Jack let out a deep breath. "Henry wouldn't have gone along with this if he didn't agree now was the time to sell. It's not a bad idea, Maggie. It's good...makes perfect sense especially if you're preg—"

"Get out," she ordered as she pointed a stiff finger at the doorway, suddenly not caring two hoots in hell if she woke half of Montana.

"I'm not in, and what are you going to do in town tonight?" His eyes narrowed. "Because I'm sure you're not just going to tell BJ and Dixie about the engagement. What's going on in that head of yours?"

She picked a boot from the floor and threw it at his head. He caught it by his left ear. "Why in the world would I tell you what I'm going to do? So you can sabotage my ideas and force me to live where you think best and you won't worry about me? I worried about you for twenty years, Jack. *Twenty years!* You can deal with it. You're a cop. Heck, you can deal with anything."

"You're sleep deprived." He wiggled his eyebrows and added in a lower, seductive tone, "Let me take you to bed. We'll talk about this there."

She felt her eyebrows rise to her hairline and her blood pressure soar. "*Sex.* Is that your answer to everything? I'm fighting for my home and all you're thinking about is—"

"You're ruining this for Henry. He'll realize something's up with us yelling like a couple of air-raid sirens."

"Henry will think we're arguing the way exes do. He's so in love he's not concerned about anything else, and that's the way it should be for him, but not me."

"But what about us trying to get back together? Selling the ranch would be prefect for that, just as Henry said. You can't live here alone. You can't run Sky Notch by yourself."

"Who do you think's been doing the running for three years now? Donald Trump? And if us getting back together involves me giving up the ranch, then there is no us—just you and what you want."

"The ranch is going to be sold, Maggie. You should get used to it and consider the good points. You'll be safe, you won't have to work so hard, and there won't be all this stress."

"You're the one complaining about all that, not me." She threw her other boot and he caught it midair, his reflexes saving his thick head again. "And I'm forty. I don't have to get used to anything." She picked up a slipper and took aim.

"All right, all right." He stepped back. "I'm going before all your shoes wind up in the hallway or plastered against my head. But would you at least think about moving to town before you completely discard the idea?"

"Sure, just like you'd think of not being a cop and moving from Chicago." She slammed the door shut in his face and tossed the slipper at it for all she was worth. *"Damn you, Jack Dawson."*

Damn him for wanting to sell Sky Notch, for putting the idea in Henry's head and for wanting to make love to her no matter what. How could Jack be so insensitive? How could he not realize this was her life and she wasn't going to give it up because it suited everyone else?

She showered and yanked on a nightshirt. She needed sleep. Tonight she'd get busy and find Andy. It wasn't that she minded Henry's selling the ranch so much as his not giving her time to prepare. The only way for her to save the ranch was to buy it from him. For that, she had to get a loan. No bank would lend her a penny until she got Andy back, got her herd together, presented a business plan and found out who the heck was trying to do her in, then stop them before they succeeded.

She gazed out her bedroom window to the hills beyond. A sob caught in her throat and she put her hand to her mouth to stifle it. She couldn't let all this go. She couldn't lose her home, the ranch she loved, Butterfly, Cisco, the other horses she'd fed and watered and taken care of all these years. This was their home, too.

Somehow, some way, she'd save Sky Notch. Not for Henry or even Ben. Their lives were somewhere else. She'd save Sky Notch for herself.

THE MOON ROSE over the Beartooth Mountains as Maggie parked in front of the Cut Loose. Not one of her usual haunts—like Dixie's—but not completely off Maggie's radar screen, either. A Black Star Beer neon sign glowed in one window, Budweiser and Coors in the other. The line of a song, "I may be a bad boy, but, honey, I'm a real good man," drifted out the open door.

Jack's theme song? At least he wasn't here to drive her crazy. Ben was home asleep, and then off to another graduation party tonight. The mess from the party at Sky Notch was cleared away, and Jack, his parents and Irene and Henry planned to have dinner in Billings to celebrate Henry's engagement. She'd begged off with a migraine—not all that far from the truth. As much as she wished her father happiness, she wasn't in a celebrating kind of mood until she got the ranch situation straightened out. And to do that she desperately needed to find Andy.

She wanted answers, and what better place than the local watering hole. Surely with all that was going on, someone had heard something. She pushed open the double doors and went inside. Ray, trim, sleek brown hair, great gray Stetson and body to go with it, poured drinks and cracked open long-necks behind the bar. To-night he sported a great leather vest. Everybody knew Ray and Ray knew everybody…and everything. Including how to keep his mouth shut.

Maggie perched herself on a stool and ordered a long-neck. "Sure is a busy night." She should get him talking, loosen him up a little. "Isn't that Flynn MacIntire at the far table?"

Ray handed her a beer. "Home on leave from the army. Made colonel two years ago. Got shot up pretty bad in Iraq and might be forced to resign his commission. Damn shame, that."

"Didn't Flynn want to be a soldier since kindergarten? I remember Grandma Mac sewing stripes on his navy suit when we made our first communion."

Ray grinned. Half the female population in Whistlers Bend between twenty and thirty had succumbed to that grin.

"Flynn's a great guy. Soldier all the way. He's got to find some way to stay in the army or he'll go nuts. Or drive us all nuts."

"It's easy to go nuts when you don't have what you want. Like me not having my bull. Hear anything about Andy? Anybody seen him around? Any word on who's taken him and the rest of my new herd?"

This time Ray gave her a long, silent, blank stare.

JACK STROLLED into the Cut Loose and spied his very lovely, totally pigheaded Maggie at the bar. Even though she wore traditional Wrangler jeans and a white cotton blouse, she didn't fit in. She seemed as comfortable perched on a bar stool as he would in a tutu.

He slipped to the corner and sat at the far end, hidden from Maggie behind others on stools and those milling around. He assumed his best "you don't want to mess with me" expression and ordered a long-neck. As he waited for the beer, he rubbed his hand over his five-o'clock shadow now morphed into full-blown stubble. He'd been at the sheriff's office and with Roy enough that people knew not to give him grief.

He didn't believe Maggie's story about a migraine for a second. She'd be out searching for answers to who had Andy and her cattle. That had trouble written all over it and he needed to protect her, his Maggie, even if he didn't agree with her on holding on to Sky Notch.

She headed over to Dan Pruitt, who was drinking a beer with a few cowboys. When Maggie exited, Jack threw some bills on the bar and went to Pruitt. "Got any ideas where Maggie's going? I want to catch up with her."

Dan rubbed his chin as he eyed Jack. "Woman problems?"

Jack narrowed his eyes a fraction. Pruitt sat up straight and shrugged dismissively. "Hell, you don't have to get all pissy. She's hunting for Butch. Seems to think he's the one who poached her bull. Messing around with the cattle industry ticks him off big-time."

"And what's your take on this?"

Dan leaned back in his chair. "The Morans have the Midas touch—everyone knows that. They have for years. They got to try something to keep in the cattle game and the beefalo idea just might work for them, or not. Butch is over at Dusty's, playing poker. There's an alley between the drugstore and that women's shop. Bet Butch has Andy and Maggie's cattle stashed at his ranch up on Red Rock. Just across the way from my spread. He's jealous as all get out over Maggie and her big ranch."

Jack strode to the door. *This was just great.* It was night and someone was after Maggie, so what does she do? Walk down a back alley.

He spied her going that way and kept his distance, cursing the fact he couldn't just be with her to protect her. She wouldn't go for that at all. A dog chased a cat across the narrow street, lined with boxes from Pretty in Pink and crates from Daily Market. Dim lights silhouetted Maggie's figure—full breasts, shapely hips, firm derriere.

Heat settled in his groin; lust fogged his brain. If he walked faster he'd catch up with her. He'd back her into the shadows and pin her against some wall or side of a building. He'd kiss her, feel her heated bare flesh against his palms, make himself part of her. Get himself beaten to pulp if he tried any of those things. Wanting to sell the ranch she loved was not a great aphrodisiac.

She darted down another alley and he followed, trying to be quiet. Boots were not made for quiet. She came to a wood porch bedecked with tired strands of red chili pepper lights and used auto parts. She stepped around an old carburetor and a stack of rusting hubcaps.

"Butch," Maggie said as she drew up to the porch.

"I hear you got my buffalo and my cattle and I want them back."

Jack rolled his eyes. Did the woman ever hear of diplomacy? Sometimes the direct approach was not the best approach…like now, with four big bad-asses playing poker and swilling beer and looking none too friendly. Being called a cattle rustler could do that to a guy.

Butch stood and glared at Maggie, his eyes dark, his stance dangerous. Jack got closer, staying in the shadows but where Butch could see him.

Butch caught sight of Jack and stepped back. "Hell, I don't have your damn cattle, Moran. Bet you've been talking to Pruitt. He's nuts. He'd say anything to get me in trouble. He thinks that because his ranch is failing, mine should, too, and so should yours and everyone's. The man has no business sense and it's driving him crazy that some of us are making a go of ranching and he isn't."

Maggie folded her arms. "Sounds to me like you're just switching the blame away from you onto Pruitt. Why should I believe you?"

Butch smirked. "Because your ornery ex-husband over there will clean my clock if I give you any trouble, and I'm getting too old for that stuff. I just want to raise cattle, play a little five-card stud and drink beer."

Busted! Jack thought as Maggie swung around and spotted him. She muttered something very unladylike, then walked over to him and growled, "What are *you* doing here?"

"I'm good at backup, remember." He flashed his

most endearing smile. The one that got him extra fries at the drive-through and a great table at a restaurant. Too bad Maggie wasn't handing out fries or tables.

Butch reclaimed his seat. "Take your lovers' quarrel somewhere else. We're playing poker here."

Jack got Maggie's arm and ushered her down the alley, away from the deck, as she said, "You're supposed to be eating dinner with Dad and Irene and your parents."

Her eyes narrowed and she stopped dead. "You were at the Cut Loose, too, weren't you? That's how you knew where I was. You followed me." She kicked a rock across the alley. "I don't need your help, especially when you want nothing more than to see me fail and the ranch to go up for sale."

He took her shoulders in his hands and looked into her deep blue eyes—blue eyes that had made him cut the right wire in that bank in Chicago. "Someone's got it in for you, Maggie. You need all the help you can get. I'm trying to help."

"And you'll get involved, save the day and think it gives you the right to run my life and tell me what I should and shouldn't do—which is sell Sky Notch. Go home. Let me be. I'll find Andy on my own terms."

"I think Pruitt has Andy. He's too antsy, too defensive, too ready to back you, and the story doesn't ring true."

"Maybe. Or perhaps the culprits are Angel's parents, because they don't like that Ben got Angel from them. Or maybe Butch and he's just handing us a bunch of malarkey about Pruitt to get us off his case."

"I'm not leaving you to wade through this mess on your own."

"Fine. Let's go home."

He gave her a sarcastic chuckle. "You really expect me to believe you won't be poking around for Andy any more tonight? I find that really hard to believe."

"You can believe anything you want. You can stand in this alley till doomsday, believing, for all I care. I'm going home and getting some sleep. It's been a really long day. My whole life is upside down and I'd like to bring this day to an end before anything else happens."

He tucked a strand of hair behind her ear. "It wasn't all bad."

Even in the dark alley he could tell she blushed. At least she remembered their lovemaking in the barn. He certainly did. "You really *are* going home?"

"Yes. Home. Now. Tomorrow I'll nose around more. Maybe Roy has some ideas or some news or something I can use. Tonight I just want a long hot bubble bath, a glass of good wine and sleep."

"Bubble bath?" His eyes met hers as they both remembered the last time one of them was in the tub.

"Forget it, Jack."

"Impossible, Maggie."

She stepped around him and traipsed down the alley as Jack stared after her. *Dang.* He'd love a bubble bath with Maggie, but that wasn't about to happen anytime soon.

Jack followed her home in the minivan—oh, how he missed his Jeep!—the lights reflecting against the Suburban bumper as Maggie sped through the darkness. He felt more at ease with her than with anyone else on earth. Even when they disagreed, like now about the ranch. What was so damn special about a ranch?

The stars formed a blanket around him, and he sniffed the fresh cool air streaming into the van. He watched the mountain peaks silhouetted in the moonlight. Okay, the wide-open spaces were incredible, but she could be a part of all this from town, right? She didn't have to live in the boonies. She didn't have to run a ranch all alone to be happy. And, if she moved to town, she'd be safe there. That was the most important thing. *Safe!*

When they reached the ranch, lights blazed from the kitchen. *Good grief. Now what?* He parked the van and got out as Maggie did the same. "Whatever's going on in there is not good. I didn't expect the parents home so soon. Dinner shouldn't be over this fast. Ben had a party tonight. What now?"

She shrugged. "Maybe it's just a burglar." She nodded as if agreeing with herself. "I can handle a burglar. Any more personal problems and I'm toast."

He wrapped his arm around her and kissed her hair, glad he was here so they could face whatever together. "I hate to tell you, but burglars don't light up the place like church at Easter."

"Maybe it's a burglar with bad eyesight." She didn't pull away but stayed beside him. "Least, I hope so."

He followed her into the house, down the hall and into the kitchen. Ben sat at the table, alone, a letter in front of him. He grinned, but it was forced, as if a glitch existed. Jack eyed Maggie. She didn't need glitches tonight.

She sat at the table across from Ben. "I thought you had another party to go to. Are you all right?"

Jack leaned against the counter. Whatever the issue, it was mostly between Maggie and Ben. Ben said, "I've been waiting for you to come home." He studied one parent, then the other. "I got a letter. It came yesterday and I forgot to open it with all the commotion around here." He held up the paper. "It's good news, Mom, really good news."

"You won a scholarship?"

"I've been accepted into the criminal justice school at the University of Denver." He grinned till the happiness covered half his face. "I'm going to be a cop like Dad."

Chapter Eleven

For the second time that day, Maggie felt as though someone had pushed her off a high cliff and the ground was fast approaching. Bad karma in the kitchen. Nothing good had happened here all day. Even her biscuits had burned. *How could Ben give up business school to be a cop?* She had to stay calm, cool, rational. She turned to him and said, *"Have you lost your flipping mind!"*

"I don't want you to worry, Mom. I'll be a good cop, as good as Dad…least, I'll try to, and nothing will happen to me. I want to help people like I did Angel. Get them to turn their life around. And I can do that as a cop. They don't *just* throw people in jail."

"Yeah, they get shot at and beat up and threatened and disarm bombs in their free time! This is a really bad idea, Ben."

Ben reached across the table and took Maggie's shaky hand in his big, strong one. "There're other parts, too."

Maggie prayed for strength not to wring his neck…or kick him in the butt and tell him he was an imbecile.

"But…but you'll make a wonderful business person, or a teacher. Ever think about being a teacher?"

"Me? School?"

"What about social work? You can work in a clinic or halfway house and help people there."

"The first line of defense is the police. They see life as it is on the streets and save a lot of people. I want to do that."

On the streets… Maggie looked at her incredibly handsome, idealistic son and her heart cracked. How could she let him go for something like *this? How could she not?* It was his life, his decision…*but he was her son, dammit. Her son.*

Jack came over and laid his hand on Ben's shoulder. "This is tough on your mom. Why don't you go to your party and give her time to adjust."

Maggie growled, "Thirty years should do it."

Ben stood and came around the table. He put his arms around her. "It's okay, Mom. I'm going to be okay. Dad's fine. Grandpa Dawson's fine. I'll be fine, too. Carry on the family tradition."

"Business is a terrific family tradition. You could start that one."

"But it's not what I want to do. I can't help it."

She heard him walk off, his gym shoes padding across the tile floor. When the door closed, she jumped up and grabbed the cast-iron skillet from the stove.

"You're going to cook? Now?"

She faced Jack, holding the pan like an ax. "*I'm going to beat you to a pulp, Jack Dawson.* How could you do this? First you get Dad to sell the ranch, then you talk Ben into being a policeman?"

"I what?"

She stepped forward; he retreated. "For years Ben's listened to all the cop stories and all the macho stuff from you and Edward, and now those stories come home to roost and Ben's going to be cop. *Blast your male macho hide.*"

She darted at him and he darted around the other side of the kitchen table. "They were just stories, Maggie. You're overreacting."

She waved her skillet. "Well, they were obviously one heck of a lot more interesting than you thought. My one-and-only son wants to be a cop. A policeman. Target practice for anyone with a gun."

"It's not that bad."

"I was the one in the hospitals with you. Don't tell me it's not bad. It's terrible." She rounded the far end of the table as Jack rounded the other. "You can run, but you can't hide."

"Sure I can. This is a big ranch."

"When Ben was three I bought him a little Fisher-Price cash register and said, 'You're going to be this.' Did I let him watch any police shows? No! Never. Wouldn't even let him make those little policeman hats in kindergarten. *And now he's going to police school.*"

"Criminal justice."

"Whatever." Two tears slid down her cheeks.

Jack's eyes widened to half his face. "*Don't cry, Maggie.* Oh, God, please don't cry."

The phone rang. He threw his hands in the air. "Good God. Now what."

She leaned on the table. "Maybe it's a telemarketer. I really hope it's a telemarketer. Tonight I would enjoy talking to a telemarketer."

He snagged the phone, barked hello and told Henry he'd be there right away. He replaced the receiver. "The fearsome foursome are in the pokey."

Maggie let go of the skillet and it hit the tile floor with a crash. "Jail? *All* of them? How'd they pull *that* off?"

"Something about a parking ticket and a sheriff mouthing off to Irene and my mom. I think the Billings riot squad was involved."

Maggie plopped down next to the skillet on the floor. Jack pointed to it. "You're not going to use that, are you?"

"Don't have the strength."

He hunkered down next to her. "I'll go bail out the parents. You get yourself together. Call BJ and Dixie. Tell them to bring Snickers."

She stared straight ahead. "You know, I thought when I finally got Ben through high school and into college the worst was over. I could kick back, relax, have free investment advice for the rest of my life. What the hell happened?"

"Hormones and free will. Least you didn't have a girl. She'd want to run a ranch by herself and chase rustlers."

She gave Jack an evil look.

He kissed her on the forehead, stood and strode across the kitchen. He stopped at the entrance to the hall and turned back. His gaze met hers. "For the record, I don't want Ben to be a cop any more than you do. Just like my dad didn't want me to be a cop."

He closed his eyes, pinched the bridge of his nose and let out a long, audible sigh. "This is not what I wanted at all," he added in a quiet, tortured voice. "I'm sorry. From the bottom of my heart I'm sorry, Maggie, that I ever put you through this kind of hell, where you worry every minute of every day about the person you love. I had no idea." Then he left.

When the door closed, she leaned back against the cabinets. Jack was always the one in control, the rational one, the go-to guy…just like Ben. *Except now.* Terror and dread ate at the core of his being just as it ate at hers.

More tears slid down her cheeks. Ben would be in terrible danger and they both knew it. Whereas Jack didn't fear for his own life, he did for his son's and had no idea what to do about it.

She wanted to crawl upstairs and pretend today had never happened. But forty-year-old women didn't crawl, they didn't whine—at least, not often—and they didn't turn to someone to fix their problems.

They were the ones everyone turned to.

She had a lifetime—or at least half a lifetime—of experience to draw from, and she'd get through this just as she'd gotten through her mother's death, Henry's heart attack, Ben's broken leg, chicken pox and car wrecks. And her divorce from Jack.

She stood, opened the cupboard and stuffed blue Peeps into a plastic bag, then one in her mouth. Courage food.

Tonight she'd find Andy and the cattle if she had to ride from one end of Montana to the other to do it. Tomorrow she'd talk to Ben, *away* from Jack, Edward and the overload of testosterone fumes that permeated the house—to make darn sure Ben really wanted to be a cop. She'd bake a cake with a hacksaw inside for the parents, who should know better than to give a cop grief. Then she'd see Jack off to Chicago.

She loved him, no doubt about that. Always had, always would. But they shared no middle ground. Things were either his way or hers.

"Okay," Maggie said as she rounded her horse trailer, tripped over a stick at the side of the road and met BJ by her SUV. "Where's Dixie?"

Maggie clicked the light on her watch to see in the darkness. "It's eleven. We're running out of time. Pruitt isn't going to drink all night at the Cut Loose. Our time for snooping is fading fast."

BJ zipped her khaki jacket against the night chill. "You don't know Pruitt. They're going to enshrine his liver at the Smithsonian."

"You sure he was still at the bar when you left?"

"*Yes, yes, yes.* For the millionth time *yes,* and Ray's going to call me when Pruitt leaves."

"How'd you get him to cooperate?"

"He had a terrible case of poison ivy and I gave him some medicine. He thinks he owes me. Dixie and I will watch out for Pruitt when he passes by here and call you so you'll have plenty of time to get off his ranch."

She gave Maggie a beady-eyed look. "Jack would kill you if he knew you were going to Pruitt's hunting for Andy."

"Jack has his own set of problems."

"Heard Ben ditched business school to be cop."

Maggie stared at BJ. "How'd you know? I just found out an hour ago."

"Brenda over at the post office saw the letter from the criminal justice college. The envelope was fat, meaning an acceptance with all the paperwork."

"She got all that from an envelope?"

BJ rolled her shoulders. "And Angel told me when I stopped in for coffee. She's really a nice girl. I like her."

Maggie leaned against the Suburban. "*Kids!* I swear, if you can survive them you can survive anything."

BJ leaned beside her. "Least you got a kid."

"What's that mean?"

"I want a child."

Maggie stared at her wide-eyed. "I can lend you Ben. That will make you change your mind in a heartbeat."

BJ smiled. "I've thought about this for a long time. I want a baby. Heard you had orange juice for breakfast."

"Yeah, orange juice. As far as I know it's still orange juice." She winked at BJ. "Flynn McIntire's back in town."

BJ coughed and choked. "Oh, yeah. There's a way to change the subject. If you're thinking there's a match there, think again. The brain and the brawn? Remember high school, when I filled his football helmet with cooked oatmeal."

"I remember when he stole a pair of those granny

panties your mom made you wear, from the girls' locker room, and ran them up the flagpole."

"Ah, yes, the good old days." She eyed Maggie. "I hate the good old days, and that includes Flynn MacIntire. No husband. Just a baby. Forty's too old to have a first baby, very high-risk. I'm thinking Third World adoption."

Maggie sighed. "You sure you don't want to sign up for the Ben cure? I can send him over for a few weeks. Drive you nuts. You'll go out and buy a dog and forget the baby."

BJ bit at her thumbnail and tapped her foot.

Maggie sighed. "This is the 'I'm going to do this, come hell or high water' look. I invented that look." She hugged BJ. "Your mother will not approve. A Third World child at the country club?"

"Mother can take her approval and—"

"Good for you." Maggie laughed and held BJ tighter. "You know Dixie and I will love being aunties. We'll spoil the baby to death, so you'll have to get used to it. I'm thinking a shower at the Purple Sage. Cake, Rocky Road ice cream, Snickers."

"I'm thinking the Cut Loose with lots of beer and pizza. I don't want the baby to be a geek like me."

"You're not a geek. You're a wonderful smart doctor and I love you. So does the whole town."

"Except Flynn MacIntire."

Dixie drove her black convertible Camaro up beside them and got out. She wore commando-black with a do-rag tied around her head. "Sorry I'm late. I had to get dressed."

Maggie plucked at the bandanna. "What the heck's this?"

"Charlie's Angels wouldn't do a stakeout in a Stetson and boots. I love Charlie's Angels. I'm Sabrina. I always wanted to get into that kick-butt kind of stuff. And don't you dare roll your eyes, Maggie Moran. This is a hot outfit."

"Get your cars off on the side road and keep an eye out for Pruitt. Call me on my cell the minute you see him pass by."

Dixie displayed her binoculars and a stun gun.

Maggie pointed. "What's all this?"

"I came prepared." Dixie beamed.

Maggie rolled her eyes. "If Roy or Jack catches us they'll have a fit. Not to mention Roy will throw me in jail. But I have to make a move tonight and can't wait for him to get a search warrant. Pruitt would find out—everyone in this town finds out everything. Then he'd move Andy or sell him and goodbye bull."

BJ asked, "What happens if Pruitt comes across you on his ranch? I hear he's one mean guy these days."

"I've got my biggest horse trailer and Peeps. I load up Andy and get out. I'll give him a handful of Peeps and sing Elvis to him. He loves anything Elvis. All I need is twenty minutes tops. Tomorrow Roy can bust Pruitt because he'll have proof, and I'll get my cattle."

"And if Andy isn't there?"

"He is—I know it. Well, Jack's the one who figured it all out and when he said it, it all made sense."

Maggie got in the Suburban. She leaned out the

window. "Just call me on my cell phone if Pruitt comes by here."

Maggie put the Suburban in gear and took off down the road. She turned into Pruitt's driveway. Gravel crunched under the tires and she slowed to accommodate the deep ruts. A dim light illuminated the front of the dark house and the barn entrance. So far, so good.

She drove the rig up to the barn, half-painted with a fresh coat of red, and killed the engine. Then she grabbed a flashlight and got out, remembering the red paint on the wire cutters. "Bingo."

She started for the barn and an ominous growl sounded behind her. Either a dog or Pruitt on a really bad night. Slowly, she turned, and faced some huge mixed-breed hound with evil intent glowing in his eyes. "I just want my bull, okay. That's all. Then I'm out of here. When I return for the cows I'll bring meat loaf. I do good meat loaf."

He growled more. She hadn't counted on a guard dog. She forced a grin and pulled a Peep from her pocket. She bit off the blue head and chewed. "Yummy, yummy." She held it out to the hound from hell. "Want some? Andy likes them. Come and get the big surprise."

She tossed the half-eaten Peep in the air and the huge mouth framed with rows of nasty teeth opened and snapped up the marshmallow. The dog's eyes brightened. Had he just smiled? He licked his chops, wagged his tail and wandered off.

· Incredible stuff, Peeps. Did the Crocodile Hunter know about the magic of Peeps in the animal world? She slid into the barn and flashed her light around. Nothing…except a huge hole in the side of the barn, about the size of a big bull buffalo? Peep packages littered the barn floor.

Did Pruitt really believe he could keep a buffalo in a barn? She giggled. Oh, Andy in a barn must have been all kinds of fun. She went to the hole, walked through and came out on the other side at a pen, its rails silhouetted by the moonlight. A large pen, not well-made, and held in place with many bales of hay and two-by-fours propped against it for extra support. She directed her light into the pen and saw… "*Andy!* There you are. Omigosh! You've grown! You're so handsome. I missed you so."

He swung his huge shaggy head her way and grunted something that sounded remarkably like *It's about damn time.*

She put down the flashlight, tugged work gloves from her back pocket and leaned on the railing, feeling all smug and triumphant. *She'd done it!* She'd found Andy. And now she'd save Sky Notch. She glanced around. Pruitt's place was a mess. It needed a lot of work, but it was still salvageable.

Why had he stolen Andy and her cattle? Good question, and tomorrow she'd find out. She dragged away the bales of hay keeping the gate in place and slid the bolt. "There's my baby," she cooed. "Are you okay? We're going to get you out of here and home where you belong."

"I don't think so." Pruitt's voice came from behind her.

Prickles of fear ran up and down her spine and her

hair stood on end. Where the heck was the warning call? Dixie hadn't worn that getup for nothing...had she? What had gone wrong? She turned. "What are you doing here?"

"That should be my line, shouldn't it?" Pruitt stood tall, legs akimbo. He was clearly pissed.

Anger over his taking Andy and her cattle overpowered her fear. Maggie gave Pruitt a beady-eyed stare and put her hands on her hips. "I'm here for my buffalo and I'm not leaving without him."

"That can be arranged."

JACK PARKED the van at Sky Notch, got out and considered the cell phone in his hand. What the hell was that call all about? He'd answered it and someone had yelled, "He's coming. Get out of there fast," then disconnected. Who would call him with a message like. Who was on the other end? He studied the phone more closely. What did it...

"Holy cow! This is Maggie's phone," he said. He slammed his hand on the hood and kicked the dirt. "Damn that woman! What is she up to now? *Get out* of where?"

The horse trailer was gone and so was the Suburban. "Andy! Pruitt! Ah, hell!" Like a gullible old fool, he'd bought Maggie's scam of going home to take a bubble bath. She'd planned to get him off guard, make him think she was innocent, then go after Andy. And he'd told her who had him. He'd been outfoxed by a pretty face and sexy body.

He pulled up the call log on the cell phone and redialed. "Who is this?"

"Who wants to know?" answered the callee. "Are you handsome, unattached, over thirty?"

"Dixie?"

"Jack? How'd you have my cell phone number? Is everything all right?"

"Maggie and I mixed up our phones. She has my cell. I have hers. I got your call."

"Omigod! Omigod! Maggie's at Pruitt's. The call was to get her out of there because he was on his way. Pruitt must be there by now."

"Pruitt's place is over on Red Rock, right?"

"BJ and I have got to save her. She'd save us."

"*No!* Stay put. I'll..." He was talking to a dead phone. He swore like he'd never sworn before, and that was going some. He jumped into the van, did a U-turn in the driveway and tore back to the road, spewing gravel in his wake. He floored the van, not that it did much good, and punched up Roy's number on the cell. He told Roy what was going down. In reply, Jack got creative swearing western-style, with animals' hind ends and manure references freely interjected.

Jack grinned. Cops were cops no matter where they hung their hats. He made the turn onto Red Rock, barely keeping two wheels on the road. He hit the accelerator again, found a mailbox with Pruitt scrawled across the side and took the road. He slowed. Silence settled around him except for a dog howling at the moon, sure happy about something.

His headlights found BJ's SUV off to one side right in front of him. If there was no gunplay, Pruitt had met his match with the Three Musketeers. But if he did have a gun... Jack's blood ran cold.

He killed his lights, pulled beside the SUV and cut the engine. Then he crept toward the barn, keeping to the brush, insects serenading him as he went. A half-moon hung over the mountains. He hunkered down to blend with the landscape as much as possible. As he got closer he spied Maggie's truck and horse trailer. A voice came from around back. Maggie's.

He moved through the darkest shadows by the barn and inched his way around the side. A light on the barn illuminated Maggie as she stood by a pen, Pruitt in front of her, rifle poised. A hand closed over Jack's shoulder and twenty years of police work kicked in as he caught a glimpse, saw a commando outfit and nailed Dixie in a choke hold.

BJ screamed. Dixie's eyes shone bright with terror, then she grinned and croaked, "Nothing like a man who knows what he wants."

A beam from a flashlight zeroed in on all three of them. Jack blinked against the sudden brightness and Pruitt said, "Get over here, all of you, if you intend for Maggie to stay healthy."

Jack nodded at Dixie. "Why are you dressed like that?"

"I always dress the part. It's part of my mystique."

BJ let out a deep sigh and plucked a sticker from her perfectly pressed slacks. "We'd better do what the man with the rifle says. I apologize for screaming. I'm not good at confrontation."

Dixie huffed, "Unless you're in your office. Then

you're one pushy woman. And I still say my cholesterol is not too high."

The three of them stood beside Maggie. Jack shook his head at Pruitt. "Put the gun down. You can't shoot us all."

Pruitt's eyes were glazed; he shifted his weight from foot to foot. He spat in the bushes. "Doesn't matter to me what happens now. My ranch is gone. I'd planned on selling Maggie's cows and calves and Andy to buy me a little more time to figure things out."

"Why me?" Maggie asked.

Pruitt's face drew into hard lines, his eyes clouded more with sadness than danger. "'Cause you get all the breaks. Figured you had it coming, being so uppity with your fancy beefalo idea. I even figured out how you controlled Andy. Charlene at Candies and Cream told me. Who would have thought."

He shook his head. "But it's all over with now. All my dreams."

BJ said, "Then let us go. This is bad for your heart, Dan, you know that."

"I don't care about my damn heart. Can't afford the medicine anyway. You all have the luck. Me? I'm a washed-up cowboy trying to make it on a mortgaged-to-the hilt ranch."

From the corners of his eyes, Jack watched Maggie ease a handful of blue Peeps from her pocket. She tossed one into the pen.

"What are you doing, Moran?" Pruitt groused.

"Feeding Andy. Keeping him happy." She nodded at

the hole in the back of the barn. "We don't want Andy upset, right? You seen what he's like when he's upset, right?" She gave Jack a quick look and tossed in another Peep, one closer to the gate. Andy wandered over and gobbled the treat.

Pruitt's hair hung in his face. His shoulders stooped and his hands shook. He swiped his nose with his shirt-sleeve, a man at the end of his rope, driven to the brink and probably not thinking straight. He said, "My ranch is everything to me."

"Maybe we can help you," Jack offered, using his hostage-negotiating skills and realizing he really did want to help Pruitt if he could. He also needed to get the man's attention off Maggie. She was up to some-thing. Wasn't she always?

"Why would you go and do that?" Pruitt studied Jack. Maggie dropped a big handful of the marshmal-lows outside the gate, their blue crystal sugar coating glittering. Andy snorted, pawed the ground, bent his head and charged the gate.

Maggie jumped back, yanking BJ and Dixie with her. Jack dodged the gate as it swung wide, but it caught Pruitt in the gut, knocking him onto his back, sending the rifle skittering across the dirt.

Jack snagged the rifle. A siren wailed in the distance. Andy scarfed Peeps, grunted, tossed his big shaggy head—had he just burped?—and trotted his one-ton brown-and-black girth off into the night.

Maggie jumped up. "You get your sorry behind back here, Andy Moran, you blasted ungrateful critter. Don't you dare run away from me. I just saved your unappre- ciative hide." She stomped her foot and yelled, "No more Peeps for you. *Men!*"

The siren stopped by the barn. The blue and yellow lights strobed into the darkness, casting a surreal qual- ity over the Montana peacefulness.

Roy hustled in, gun drawn. He zeroed in on Pruitt, still on the ground, Jack, then Dixie. His head snapped back. "What's with you?"

Dixie straightened her do-rag and fluffed the little curls at each side. "Oh, for heaven's sake. So I'm not wearing a Stetson and boots or my waitress garb. I'm dressed for action. See?" She held up her arms. "One of these days someone with zing will come to this town. Right now there's no pizzazz, no fun, no—"

"Insanity?" Roy offered.

Maggie went to Pruitt. She smiled and reached out her hand. "Let me help you up, Dan. You must have tripped."

Chapter Twelve

Roy glanced around. "Where the heck's Andy?"

Maggie considered Pruitt, a man alone, who'd lost everything dear to him. Defeated. "Well, Roy," Maggie started to say. "it's the darnedest thing. Dan here found Andy wandering around and put him in this pen for me. I came over to pick him up."

She shrugged. "But wouldn't you know, Andy's escaped again. And just when I was going to let Dan borrow Andy to get a herd of his own going. This is a great ranch for beefalo."

Roy holstered his gun and tipped his hat to the back of his head. "What the hell's going on, Maggie?"

Pruitt didn't move, but looked at Maggie, dumbfounded as she continued, "Dan's going to sell off some of his acreage to get cash for young cows. Andy's got enough *bull* in him for both our herds till they get bigger, so I don't mind sharing. Beefalo's really taking off around the country. Guess the conglomerates aren't going to gobble up *all* the ranches after all. Right, Dan?

"I know what it's like to love your ranch, to be desperate enough to do *anything* to keep it. We're going to be all right, Dan. My ranch and yours. We're going to make this work. We're going to keep our homes."

Jack came over, draped his arm around her shoulders and kissed her forehead. "We should head back to Sky Notch. We can start hunting for Andy in the morning."

Dan stood in front of Maggie and Jack, blocking their way. "I…I don't rightly know what to say."

Maggie smiled and touched his arm. "You'll come up with something when you return those cows you *borrowed* from me. Do you need help?"

He wagged his head. "My two brothers over in Livingston helped me borrow them, and were none too thrilled about doing it, either. They'll be plumb tickled this time."

Jack held out his hand to shake Dan's. "I wish you luck. We can all use luck."

Dan grinned, seeming years younger. "Thanks. I think I just got more than my share of it tonight."

Dixie walked up and spread her arms wide, encompassing the whole scene. "Well, for Whistlers Bend this was a pretty exciting night." She flipped off her bandanna and her curls sprang out as if happy to be free. "We could do with more nights like this."

Maggie glared and BJ growled, *"Forget it!"*

Dixie huffed. "You all are a bunch of sissies. Someday—"

BJ took Dixie's arm and hauled her toward the driveway saying, "Someday Hans Solo will swoop down in his Millennium Falcon, whisk you away and make you the happiest woman on Earth."

Jack followed Maggie to her rig. He opened the door to the Suburban, then closed her safely inside. He leaned into the window. "I'm going to watch you turn around and head down the driveway and I'm going to follow you. For both our sakes, just go home. Don't stop, don't pass go, don't collect two hundred dollars. Just go home."

She kissed him, his warm sensual lips against hers a touch of Montana paradise. His tongue leisurely exploring her mouth gave her chills, then intense heat rippled through her body. What this man did to her equilibrium was sinful beyond words. She drew back slowly, sucking his lower lip into her mouth in an arousing kiss.

His heated look stole her breath away. "I should jump in there with you and finish this off in a proper manner."

"We're in Pruitt's driveway. He's in his house, about twenty feet away."

"He won't care."

She gently pushed at Jack's chest. "Go. I'll wait for you at the end of the driveway." She smiled and shook her head. "I can't believe I forgot to ask what happened to the parents. Are they still in the slammer?"

Jack grinned, making her want to kiss him again. "I sprang them. More accurately, Roy and I did. He called in a favor and I made a contribution to the Little League fund."

"Wish I had pictures." She laughed. "But they're home now, right?"

"Celebrating their freedom at the Cut Loose. They're getting to be regulars." Jack put his hands to his hips.

"How'd we get into this? Ben? The parents? So much responsibility, so little appreciation."

"We're middle-aged, *middle* being the operative word. And, I think our parents are secretly getting back at us for all the grief we caused them."

"Grief? Me? Nah!" Jack stepped back. "Don't get lost."

Maggie fired the engine and circled the rig in the driveway then headed for Red Rock. Jack trailed behind her. She could see the minivan from her side mirror, his arm resting on the door, elbow hooked outside. She caught his silhouette behind the wheel. Tall, strong, definitive features...and she knew every one of them intimately. His forehead, which wrinkled when he worried; his dark eyes, which were whiskey-brown when he was relaxed and black as the night when he was making love. His nose, broken more times than she realized; his determined chin, delectable lips, broad shoulders, muscled chest and abs.

Manly attributes guaranteed to please. She pressed down the window, letting the cool night air stream over her heated skin.

When she drove into Sky Notch, she stopped by the barn, Jack aiming the van right beside her. She slid from the Suburban and went to him as he got out. She threw her arms around him and kissed him, giving him a bit of her own skilled tongue. He snagged her in his arms, lifting her off the ground.

"I want you, Jack," she breathed against his lips. "Right now. I don't care about tomorrow and the future. Just now."

He set her down and smoothed back her hair as he gazed into her eyes. "I'm not going anywhere near that house, especially the kitchen."

She laughed and grasped his hand, then led him toward the barn. There, she climbed the ladder into the loft and slumped into a mound of hay that faced the big open doors framing stars and a moon set in an ink-black sky that stretched till the end of time. She was home.

Jack sat down beside her. "Listen," he whispered. "An owl? Sounds really close."

Maggie snuggled up next to him, wrapping her arm around his middle. "We're in a barn. This is his turf. When I first came home I'd put Ben to bed and walk out here and gaze at the sky. Somehow it was comforting to know it covered both you and me. I'd find a star and think you'd be looking at the same one and we were connected, even though we were hundreds of miles apart."

He rolled over on top of her, peering into her eyes, his desire for her nestled intimately between her legs. He kissed her. "God, I love you, Maggie. I have since the day I saw you on Michigan Avenue. Our being together like this or apart in Chicago and Montana doesn't change how much I love you. Nothing can change that. You are the air I breathe, the reason I exist."

Then he made love to her as a husband makes love to his wife—with his body, his mind and his soul.

She watched the moon rise higher into the night sky. They talked and made love again, then she fell asleep in Jack's arms, and stayed there till the first rays of sun flooded the loft.

She felt around for him, but he was gone—she knew it as much in her heart as by feeling the empty spot beside her—and the sensation of not having Jack by her was nearly more than she could stand. Slowly, she opened her eyes, the full force of being alone crashing down around her. She sat up, pulled her legs to her chest and wrapped her arms around them. Last night with Jack was wonderful. But it couldn't last. Nothing that terrific lasted forever. Life didn't work like that.

Jack was a Chicago cop with every fiber of his being, and Sky Notch was her heart, her world. There was simply no way for her and Jack to compromise. She understood that and she accepted it, because at forty she knew when to fight and when to let go. The only thing left to fight for now was Sky Notch. That meant she had to find Andy. And she would.

But for a moment she needed to savor the memory of being with her husband. Jack would never be an ex, not really. They were bound by an incredible love that would never end.

FOUR HOURS LATER she trudged into the Purple Sage, mussed hair, dirty jeans—and still no sign of Andy.

"Good Lord!" Dixie splashed coffee on the table as Maggie slid into her usual booth. "What the heck happened to you? And you had the nerve to criticize my commando outfit last night. Is this your scarecrow outfit?"

"Andy happened." She held up her mug. "Pour."

"Orange juice?" Dixie grinned.

She eyed Dixie. "Coffee. As of this morning. Coffee."

"Pity. I was getting used to orange juice." Dixie tipped the pot as Maggie said, "Dan Pruitt and I chased that no-good, conniving, sneaky piece of tough bull steak through the McClouds' pasture, down three creeks, through Denise Patterson's clothesline, complete with fresh wash—ever see a buffalo in a flannel nightgown?—into BJ's prize rose garden…could be the end of a beautiful friendship—up one alley and down the other and then back out of town. Then I had a meeting with the bank, so I had to give up the chase."

She lifted her mug in triumph. "But life is not all thorns. The bank gave me a loan for Sky Notch."

"With you looking like that?"

"Guess they saw me as a working girl. They asked no questions. Just had me sign a paper. Now I can buy Dad out. I think they have faith in this beefalo idea."

"Or they have faith in Jack Dawson."

Maggie felt her eyes widen and her heart almost stop.

"Close your mouth, dear. Bernie, the clerk at the bank, was in here earlier. Blueberry pie can get a guy to tell you most anything."

Maggie jumped up. "I'm going to kill him."

"Bernie's got a wife, two kids, three cats. Reconsider."

Maggie sneered at Dixie. "Not Bernie. *Jack.* He's doing it all over again. Running my life, and this is the perfect way. He'll put money in Sky Notch and that will give him a say—a really big say—in what goes on."

"Have you told him about the *coffee* yet?"

"I haven't seen him yet. But as soon as I do—"

"There's something else you should know. Jack asked Angel to move in with you at Sky Notch."

Dixie put her hand on Maggie's shoulder. "He's trying to help. He doesn't want you to be alone, Maggie, and when he and Ben and your father leave, you will be alone."

Alone. The word sat in her gut like a hunk of lasagna eaten at midnight. She shook her head. "He's trying to control me. That's what this is all about. It's still that cop thing. If he's not in charge he's not happy."

"Angel's a good person. You won't be sorry."

"But he never *asked* me."

Dixie nodded out the window. "The man in question's heading into Roy's office right now. No homicide, okay. You'll have a witness. It *is* the sheriff's office."

Maggie stood. She fished money out of her pocket, put it on the table, then headed for the door. "Make a call and get Roy out of the office. It's for his own protection."

Maggie stormed across the street. Roy sat behind his desk, Jack across from him. She faced Jack. "How dare you."

Roy got to his feet. "Okay, that's my cue. I need a caffeine fix. Remember this is taxpayers property. Try to save the pieces."

He strolled to the door and Maggie frowned at Jack. "You bought into Sky Notch. You think you're going to force me to sell and move into town, don't you." She tossed her head. "I'm not doing it. I am not pregnant, so you do not have to worry about that and—"

He stood and she had to back up. "I wasn't worried about you being pregnant, except the way fathers and husbands always worry. It took some getting used to, but I was…excited."

He shrugged his broad shoulders. "But if you're not pregnant, that's okay, too. My putting up the collateral for the ranch has nothing to do with you selling the place or you being pregnant."

"You expect me to believe that?"

"Yes, dammit, I do. I've never lied to you. And why would I ask Angel to move out to Sky Notch if I wanted you to sell? Does that make any sense?"

"Right now nothing makes sense." She ran her hand over her face and exhaled. "You're right. I'm sorry. You don't lie. And why did you ask Angel to move in with me? So what if I'm alone? A lot of people are alone."

"Angel deserves a good home and we owe her." He wagged his eyebrows. "She talked Ben out of going into criminal justice, at least right now. Said he needed to give business school a shot since he loves the ranch and might need to know how to manage it someday. But if he hated business and still wanted to be a policeman that was okay, too."

"Maybe I should build Angel her own house in the west pasture. Bet she'd like a Jacuzzi, a car, maybe a swimming pool with a diving board, stuff like that."

"I think she'll be thrilled with free room and board. She's taking art classes three days a week in Billings. Maybe we could spring for a used car."

She stared at Jack. "I get that you don't intend for me

to sell Sky Notch. So why *did* you put up the money? *That* I don't understand. Now that I have Andy back, eventually, I can get the loan on my own."

His face sobered and he paced. "It's an investment. The property's good, the beefalo idea's sound, the manager's the Bill Gates of the beefalo world. What more can I ask for?"

He stopped pacing. Something in his eyes suggested he *did* want more. *He wanted her.* That was what this was all about. Jack Dawson, the man who could face anything couldn't make this work between them. They'd split thirteen years ago because neither of them would change and he didn't want that to happen again.

Well, neither did she. She was different; *they* were different. Not just older but far wiser. She took his hand and entwined her fingers with hers. "Don't go."

"But—"

"Run for sheriff. Cyrus is still recuperating in Florida and probably intends to continue doing that with a fishing pole in his hand for the rest of his life. Roy is content to be deputy—he's made that clear."

"But—"

"I realize this is not Chicago, but there are problems here. We still don't know where those wide tire tracks at Silver Gulch came from. And the big trucks that are suddenly on the roads in the middle of the night—we don't have a clue what that's about, either. Just *try* living here. No strings. Don't give up your apartment in Chicago. Take a leave of absence from the force. I'll give you Butterfly. We don't have to live together if that's too much pressure, but you can have a mutual say in Sky Notch. You can stay in town. Dixie will make sure you have lemon meringue pie every day. If you still don't like it in Whistlers Bend you can leave. I won't give you any grief and I'll repay the loan and—"

He pulled her into his arms and kissed her and she felt more at home there than anywhere else on earth.

"I don't remember you ever talking so much," he said against her lips.

"I have a lot to say. Thirteen years of things to say."

"I didn't think you wanted anything to do with me and law enforcement."

"I'll deal. I swear I will. If you stay I can deal with anything. I can't let you go again, Jack. Who will I grow old with? Who will I make love with in the loft?"

His eyes searched her face, reaching into her thoughts. He smiled. "Me."

She tightened her arms around him. "I love you. I can hardly breathe I love you so much."

He pulled his head back, smiling. "Marry me— again. You are a fabulous wife, Maggie, and I want you for my own again. I don't want to live without you."

"Then you won't. I'm yours—you're mine. We'll never be apart." She kissed his wonderful lips. "Who ever thought forty could be this fabulous?"

Welcome to the world of American Romance!
Turn the page for excerpts from our
September 2005 titles.
We're sure you'll enjoy every one of these books!

It's time for some BLOND JUSTICE!
Downtown Debutante *is Kara Lennox's*
second book in her series about
three women who were duped by the
same con man and vow to get revenge.
We know you're going to love this
fast-paced, humorous story!

Brenna Thompson drew herself deeper into the down comforter, trying to reclaim the blessed relief of sleep. But instead of drifting off again, she awoke with a jolt and smacked into hard reality. She was stranded in Cottonwood, Texas, without a dime to her name, her entire future hanging by a thread.

And someone was banging on her door at the Kountry Kozy Bed & Breakfast.

Wearing only a teddy, she slid out of bed and stumbled to the door. "I told you to take the key," she said grumpily, opening the door, expecting to see Cindy, her new roommate. "What time is it, any—" She stopped as her bleary eyes struggled to focus. Standing in the hallway was a broad-shouldered man in a dark suit, a blindingly white shirt and a shimmering blue silk tie. He was a foot taller than Brenna's own five-foot-three, and she had to strain her neck to meet his cool, blue-eyed gaze.

In a purely instinctual gesture, she slammed the door closed. My God, she was almost naked. A stranger in a suit had seen her almost naked. Her whole body flushed, then broke out in goose bumps.

The knock came again, louder this time.

"Uh, just a minute!" She didn't have a robe. She wasn't a robe-wearing sort of person. But she spied one belonging to Sonya, her other roommate, lying at the foot of her bed. The white silk garment trailed the floor, the sleeves hanging almost to Brenna's fingertips— Sonya was tall—but at least it covered her, sort of.

Taking a deep breath, she opened the door again. "Yes?"

Still there. Still just as tall, just as imposing, just as handsome. Not her type, she thought quickly. But there was a certain commanding presence about this stranger that made her stomach swoop and her palms itch.

"Brenna Thompson?"

Deep voice. It made all her hair follicles stand at attention.

"Yes, that's me." He didn't smile, and a frisson of alarm zapped through her. "Is something wrong? Oh, my God, did something happen to someone in my family?"

He hesitated. "No. I'm Special Agent Heath Packer with the FBI. This is Special Agent Pete LaJolla."

Brenna saw a second man lurking in the shadows. He stepped closer and grunted a greeting. Both men looked as if they expected to enter.

Brenna glanced over her shoulder. The room was a complete wreck. Every available surface was covered with clothes and girly stuff, not to mention baby things belonging to Cindy's little boy. Even fastidious Sonya's bed was unmade. Sonya was used to servants doing that sort of thing for her.

Special Agent No. 1 didn't wait for her consent. He eased past her into the room, his observant gaze taking everything in.

"If you'd given me some warning, I could have tidied up," she groused, pulling the robe more tightly around her. She hadn't realized how thin the fabric was.

Mustering her manners, Brenna cleared off a cosmetics case and a pair of shoes from the room's only chair. "Here, sit down. You're making me nervous. And... Agent LaJolla, was it?" She brushed some clothes off Sonya's twin bed. LaJolla nodded and sat gingerly on the bed while Brenna retreated to her own bed. She sat cross-legged on it, drawing the covers over her legs both for warmth and modesty.

"I assume you know why we're here," Packer said.

If you enjoyed Penny McCusker's
first book for American Romance,
Mad About Max *(April 2005),*
you'll be happy to hear that her second book,
Noah and the Stork, *has arrived!*
And if you haven't read her before,
you'll be delighted by Penny's warmhearted
humor in this charming story set in
the town of Erskine, Montana.

Men were generally a pain in the neck, Janey Walters thought, but there were times when they came in handy. Like when your house needed a paint job, or your kitchen floor needed refinishing or your car was being powered by what sounded like a drunk tap dancer with a thirst for motor oil.

Or when you woke in the middle of the night, alone and aching for something that went way beyond physical, into realms best left to Hallmark and American Greetings. Whoever wrote those cards managed to say everything about love in a line or two. Janey didn't even like to think about the subject anymore. Thinking about it made her yearn, yearning made her hopeful, and hope, considering her track record with the opposite sex, was a waste of energy.

She set her paintbrush on top of the can and climbed to her feet. She'd been sitting on the front porch for the past hour, slapping paint on the railings, wondering if the petty violence of it might help exorcise the sense of futility that had settled over her of late. All she'd managed to do was polka-dot everything in the vicinity—the lawn and rose bushes, the porch floor and herself—which only made more work for her and did nothing to solve the real problems.

And boy, did she have problems. No more than any other single mom who lived in a house that was a century old, with barely enough money to keep up with what absolutely had to be fixed, never mind preventative maintenance. And thankfully, Jessie was a normal nine-year-old girl—at least she seemed well-adjusted, despite the fact that her father had never been, and probably would never be, a part of her life.

It only seemed worse to Janey now that her best friend had gotten married. But then, Sara had been waiting for six years for Max to figure out he loved her, and Janey would never have wished for a different outcome. She and Sara still worked together, and talked nearly every day, so it wasn't as if anything had really changed in Janey's life. It just felt...emptier somehow.

She put both hands on the small of her aching back and stretched, letting her head fall back and breathed deeply, in and out, until she felt some of the frustration and loneliness begin to fade away.

"Now there's a sight for sore eyes."

Janey gasped, straightening so fast she all but gave herself whiplash. That voice... Heat moved through her, but the cold chill that snaked down her spine won hands down. It couldn't be him, she told herself. He couldn't simply show up at her house with no warning, no time to prepare.

"The best scenery in town was always on this street."

She peeked over her shoulder, and the snappy comebacks she was famous for deserted her. So did the unsnappy comebacks and all the questions she should've been asking. She couldn't have strung a coherent sentence together if the moment had come with subtitles. She was too busy staring at the man standing on the other side of her wrought-iron fence.

His voice had changed some; it was deeper, with a gravelly edge that seemed to rasp along her nerve endings. But there was no mistaking that face, not when it had haunted her memories—good and bad—for more than a decade. "Noah Bryant," Janey muttered, giving him a nice, slow once-over.

Tina Leonard continues her popular
COWBOYS BY THE DOZEN series
with Crockett's Seduction.
These books are wonderfully entertaining
and exciting. If you've never read Tina Leonard,
you're in for a treat.
After all, who can resist a cowboy—
let alone twelve of them!
Meet the brothers of Malfunction Junction
and let the roundup of those
Jefferson bad boys begin!

Even now, at his brother Bandera's wedding, Crockett Jefferson wondered if Valentine Cakes—the mother of his brother Last's child—realized how much time he spent staring at her. His deepest, darkest secret was that she evoked fantasies in his mind, fantasies of the two of them—

"Well, that's that," his eldest brother, Mason, said to Hawk and Jellyfish, the amateur detectives and family friends who'd come to the Malfunction Junction ranch to deliver news about Maverick Jefferson, the Jefferson brothers' missing father.

Before he heard anything else, Crockett once again found his eyes glued to Valentine and her tiny daughter, Annette. Watching her was a habit he didn't want to give up, no matter how much family drama flowed around him.

Hawk looked at Mason. "Do you want to know what we learned about your father before or after you eat your piece of wedding cake?"

Crockett sighed, and took a last look at the fiery little redhead as he heard the pronouncement about Maverick. She was holding her daughter and a box of heart-shaped petits fours she'd made for Bandera's wedding reception. She smiled at him, her pretty blues eyes encouraging, her mouth bowing sweetly, and his heart turned over. With regret he looked away.

She could never know how he felt about her.

He really didn't *want* to feel the way he did about the mother of his brother's child. So, to get away from the temptation to keep staring, he followed Hawk, Jellyfish and Mason under a tree so they could talk.

"We were able to confirm that Maverick was in Alaska, for a very long time," Hawk said.

Crockett thought Mason surely had to be feeling the same excitement and relief that filled him; finally some trace of Maverick had been found.

"But we felt it was important to come back and tell you the news, then let you decide what more you need to learn," Hawk said.

Crockett felt a deep tug in his chest. Now they would hold a family council to decide what to do. It was good they'd found out now, since all the brothers were at the ranch for the annual Fourth of July gathering and Bandera's wedding.

Now that so many of the Jefferson brothers had married and moved away, Mason wanted to hold a family reunion at least twice a year—Christmas in the winter and Fourth of July in the summer. Christmas was a natural choice, but Independence Day was a time when the pond was warm enough for the children to swim, Mason had said. But Crockett knew his request really had nothing to do with pond water. Mason just wanted the brothers and their families together, on the so-called Malfunction Junction ranch, their home.

Crockett had to admit there was something to the power of family bonding as he turned to again watch Valentine with her tiny daughter.

His Wedding, *by Muriel Jensen,*
is Muriel's last book in the saga of the Abbotts,
a northeastern U.S. family
whose wealth and privilege could not shield them
from the harsher realities of life,
including a kidnapping.
At last the mystery of the kidnapping is solved—
by the missing Abigail herself,
with the help of Brian Girard, himself an Abbott child
who is soon planning his wedding!

Brian Girard sat on the top porch step of his shop at just after 6:00 a.m., drinking a cup of coffee while reading the *Losthampton Leader*. The ham-and-cheese bagel he'd bought tasted like sawdust when he saw the front-page article about Janet Grant-Abbott's move to Losthampton, and he'd thrown the bagel into the garbage.

"Long-lost heiress home again," said the caption under a photo of Janet that must have been taken on her return from Los Angeles.

From the small plane visible some distance behind her, the setting was obviously the airport. Her hair was short and fluffy, and she was squinting against the sun.

At a glance she resembled any other young woman on a casual afternoon. It was the second look that made you realize she was someone special. Her good breeding showed in the tilt of her head and the set of her shoulders; the intellect in her eyes elevated a simple prettiness to fascinating beauty.

The article revealed all the known details of her kidnap, the Abbott family's position in the world of business, her brothers' accomplishments then her own history as a successful stockbroker.

It went on to say that her adopted sister had come to Losthampton thinking she might be the missing Abbott sister, Abigail, but that a DNA test had proven she wasn't. And that had brought Janet onto the scene.

He was just about to give the reporter credit for a job not-too-badly done, when he got to the part about himself:

"Brian Girard, the illegitimate son of Susannah Steward Abbott, Nathan Abbott's first wife, and Corbin Girard, the Abbotts' neighbor, has been welcomed into the bosom of the family." It continued in praise of their generosity, considering that Corbin Girard was responsible for the fire in their home and the vandalism to the business Brian owned. It explained in detail that Brian had been legally disowned for defecting to the Abbott camp by giving the Abbotts information that stopped them from making a business deal they would have regretted. Brian has no idea how the paper had gotten that information, unless one of the family had told them.

Annoyed, he threw the newspaper in the trash, on top of the bagel, and strode, coffee cup in hand, down his dock. The two dozen boats he'd worked so hard to repair bobbed at the ends of their lines, a testament to his determination to start over at something he enjoyed.

The refinished shop was restocked with the old standbys people came in for day after day, plus a few new gourmet products, a line of sophisticated souvenirs and shirts and hats with his logo on them—a rowboat with a grocery bag in the bow—visible proof of his spirit to survive in the face of his father's continued hatred.

He could fight all the roadblocks in his path, he thought, gazing out at the sun rising to embroider the water with light, but how could he fight the truth? No matter what he did, he would always be the son of a woman who'd thrown away her husband and other two sons like so much outdated material, and of a man who'd rejected him since the day he was born.

The sorry fact was that Brian couldn't fight it. He could do his best to be honest and honorable, but he would never inspire a favorable newspaper article. Every time his name came up, it would be as the son of his reprehensible parents.

He didn't know what to do about it.

Then again, Janet Grant-Abbott wasn't sure what to do, either.

If you enjoyed what you just read,
then we've got an offer you can't resist!

Take 2 bestselling love stories FREE!

Plus get a FREE surprise gift!

Clip this page and mail it to Harlequin Reader Service®

IN U.S.A.
3010 Walden Ave.
P.O. Box 1867
Buffalo, N.Y. 14240-1867

IN CANADA
P.O. Box 609
Fort Erie, Ontario
L2A 5X3

YES! Please send me 2 free Harlequin American Romance® novels and my free surprise gift. After receiving them, if I don't wish to receive anymore, I can return the shipping statement marked cancel. If I don't cancel, I will receive 4 brand-new novels every month, before they're available in stores! In the U.S.A., bill me at the bargain price of $4.24 plus 25¢ shipping & handling per book and applicable sales tax, if any*. In Canada, bill me at the bargain price of $4.99 plus 25¢ shipping & handling per book and applicable taxes**. That's the complete price and a savings of at least 10% off the cover prices—what a great deal! I understand that accepting the 2 free books and gift places me under no obligation ever to buy any books. I can always return a shipment and cancel at any time. Even if I never buy another book from Harlequin, the 2 free books and gift are mine to keep forever.

154 HDN DZ7S
354 HDN DZ7T

Name	(PLEASE PRINT)
Address	Apt.#
City	State/Prov.	Zip/Postal Code

Not valid to current Harlequin American Romance® subscribers.

Want to try two free books from another series?
Call 1-800-873-8635 or visit www.morefreebooks.com.

* Terms and prices subject to change without notice. Sales tax applicable in N.Y.
** Canadian residents will be charged applicable provincial taxes and GST.
All orders subject to approval. Offer limited to one per household.
® are registered trademarks owned and used by the trademark owner and or its licensee.

AMER04R   ©2004 Harlequin Enterprises Limited

Catch the latest story
in the bestselling miniseries
by

Tina Leonard

Cowboys BY THE DOZEN!

Artist, rancher and bull rider Crockett Jefferson
has always been a man of strong passions. So
when he finds himself thinking passionately
about the one woman he can't have—
Valentine Cakes, the mother of his brother's
child—this sensitive cowboy knows
he's in trouble!

CROCKETT'S SEDUCTION
Harlequin American Romance #1083

Available September 2005

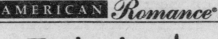
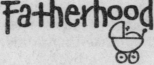